PRAISE FOR THE BOOKS OF
AGATHA AWARD-WINNING AUTHOR
EDITH MAXWELL

"The historical setting is redolent and delicious, the townspeople engaging, and the plot a proper puzzle, but it's Rose Carroll — midwife, Quaker, sleuth — who captivates in this irresistible series debut."
— Catriona McPherson, Agatha-, Anthony- and Macavity-winning author of the Dandy Gilver series

"Clever and stimulating novel . . . masterfully weaves a complex mystery."
— *Open Book Society*

"Riveting historical mystery . . . [a] fascinating look at nineteenth-century American faith, culture, and small-town life."
— William Martin, *New York Times* bestselling author of *Cape Cod* and *The Lincoln Letter*

"Intelligent, well-researched story with compelling characters and a fast-moving plot. Excellent!"
— *Suspense Magazine*

"A series heroine whose struggles with the tenets of her Quaker faith make her strong and appealing . . . imparts authentic historical detail to depict life in a 19th-century New England factory town."
— *Library Journal*

"Intriguing look at life in 19th-century New England, a heroine whose goodness guides all her decisions, and a mystery that surprises."
— *Kirkus Reviews*

BOOKS BY EDITH MAXWELL

Quaker Midwife Mysteries

Delivering the Truth
Called to Justice
Turning the Tide
Charity's Burden
Judge Thee Not
Taken Too Soon
A Changing Light

Lauren Rousseau Mysteries

Speaking of Murder
Murder on the Bluffs

Local Foods Mysteries

A Tine to Live, a Tine to Die
'Til Dirt Do Us Part
Farmed and Dangerous
Murder Most Fowl
Mulch Ado About Murder

More Books by Edith Maxwell

Country Store Mysteries
(written as Maddie Day)

Flipped for Murder
Grilled for Murder
When the Grits Hit the Fan
Biscuits and Slashed Browns
Death Over Easy
Strangled Eggs and Ham
Nacho Average Murder
Candy Slain Murder

Cozy Capers Book Group Mysteries
(written as Maddie Day)

Murder on Cape Cod
Murder at the Taffy Shop

A CHANGING LIGHT

A
QUAKER MIDWIFE
MYSTERY

EDITH MAXWELL

BEYOND THE PAGE
PUBLISHING

A Changing Light
Edith Maxwell
Beyond the Page Books
are published by
Beyond the Page Publishing
www.beyondthepagepub.com

ISBN: 978-1-954717-00-8

For reference librarians everywhere. Authors depend on you for history, for deep databases you know how to search, and for an affinity in wanting to know the facts about the past.

AUTHOR'S NOTE

The annual Spring Opening was a very real affair, bringing visitors from all over the world to view Amesbury's carriages. John Mayer, Executive Director of the Amesbury Carriage Museum, dug up newspaper notices on the Spring Opening for me. I also consulted Amesbury historian Margaret Rice's *Sun on the River: The Story of the Bailey Family Business 1856–1956* for descriptions of the week's business negotiations and nightly social events. Amesbury librarian Margie Walker has helped me find facts from the past for every book in this series, and I am grateful.

I have invented members of Amesbury's 1890 Board of Trade and make no claims about the actual board's involvement in murder, nor about Mr. Lowell's disinclination to become involved in the issues before the town, as a character claims in the book.

The Montgomery Carriage Company of Ottawa, Canada, came out of my imagination. I wish to cast no aspersions or senility on any actual Ontarian carriage manufacturer of the era.

I consulted about railroad timetables and routes with local historical train expert Peter Bryant, formerly with the Salisbury Point Railroad Association (Peter is also a docent at the John Greenleaf Whitter Home Museum). I also received maps, timetables, and other details of train travel from Richard Nichols, Carl Byron, and Archivist Rick Nowell of the Boston & Maine Railroad Historical Society, Inc. I am grateful for the help of experts, and any errors in the book are of my own doing.

Amesbury very nearly became the automobile capital of the United States. My fictional Ned Bailey's thoughts about starting a motorcar company were not complete fantasy. Some of the first electric cars in the country were made in the town by the real Bailey family from 1907 to 1915. Two still exist—and still run. Also, I imply no aspersions whatsoever on the historical Baileys, who were one of Amesbury's First Families and whose descendants still live in Amesbury and surrounding towns.

The Remedy: Robert Koch, Arthur Conan Doyle, and the Quest to Cure Tuberculosis by Thomas Goetz is an excellent reference on tuberculosis and the rise of science toward the end of the nineteenth century. I gleaned a number of helpful facts from it for this book, and it's also great reading.

I wrote this book during the Covid-19 pandemic, and I found the parallels between the scourge of TB, with its lack of either a vaccine or a cure, and the current novel coronavirus frankly terrifying.

As I've done with each book, I consulted *Miss Parloa's New Cook Book and Marketing Guide*, published in 1880, for ideas about food as well as sample menus that might have been served at the Grand Hotel. I also made use of the *Montgomery Ward & Co. Catalogue and Buyers' Guide* from 1895, Marc McCutcheon's *Everyday Life in the 1800s*, and *The Massachusetts Peace Officer: a Manual for Sheriffs, Constables, Police, and Other Civil Officers* by Gorham D. Williams, 1891.

I have taken liberties with Friend John's whereabouts. According to *John Greenleaf Whittier: a Biography* by Roland H. Woodwell, Whittier spent the entire winter and spring of 1890 with the Cartlands in Danvers, Massachusetts. I brought him back to Amesbury for this book so Rose could take counsel with her wise fFriend. Apologies to those who study his life and to my docent friends at the John Greenleaf Whittier Home Museum in Amesbury. I quote some of the lines Whitter wrote for Susan Babson Swasey, which Woodwell cites as later published in "Whittier and a Girl's Album" by Ethel Parton in *Youth's Companion*, January 23, 1896. I also reference Whittier's poem "The Meeting."

I got the quote from Annie Oakley from the Women's History Museum, but I wasn't able to verify when she said it. Her marriage in Ontario, Canada, is fact.

As always, I consulted the Online Etymology Dictionary (www.etymonline.com/) and Google Ngram Viewer for information about when particular words and phrases entered the language, as well as *The American Slang Dictionary from 1890*, originally published by James Maitland in 1891.

<u>ONE</u>

THE WORLD WAS CHANGING AROUND ME, around all of us, in this first year of the 1890s. I passed men stringing wires above Main Street in Amesbury, Massachusetts, converting the horse-drawn trolley system to one powered by electricity. Our country had four new western states. We had vaccines available for rabies, cholera, and anthrax, although — alas — not for tuberculosis or the recent scourge of Asiatic influenza.

My own small world was transforming, too. I smiled to myself on a chilly late afternoon in early Third Month as I raised my hand to knock at the door of the Orchard Street home where my elderly mentor, Orpha Perkins, lived with her granddaughter and her family. The door opened before I could lift the knocker. It wasn't Alma Latting who faced me, though, but a pleasant-looking lady in her forties. She toted a black satchel very much like my own midwifery bag.

"Oh! Good afternoon," the woman said. She adjusted a bowler decorated with a blue ribbon atop her still-blond hair. "I hope I didn't startle you."

"Not at all. I've come to call on Orpha."

The smile slid off her face. "Good." She peered more closely at my face. "Are you the midwife?"

"Yes." I extended a hand. "I'm Mrs. Rose Carroll Dodge."

Her handshake was firm. "My name is Mary Chatigny, physician. Mrs. Perkins is under my care."

"I'm pleased to meet thee, Mary. I thought that looked like a medical bag." Lady doctors weren't unheard of, but I hadn't realized one practiced here in Amesbury.

"I'm normally a tuberculosis specialist."

My eyes widened. "Does she — "

"No." She held up a hand. "Have no fear. Old age is Mrs. Perkins's infirmity, nothing more."

"I'm relieved to hear it's not the deadly wasting disease." While modern medicine had recently identified the cause of the illness, it hadn't discovered a cure other than clean air and water, as well as rest. "How did thee come to care for her?"

"She knew my late mother, Margaret Flaherty, who bound me to look out for Mrs. Perkins. I'm happy to do so. She was speaking of you just now."

"Orpha is my mentor. I took over her midwifery practice several years ago after she retired."

"Spend as much time with her as you can. While you can. Good day, Mrs. Dodge." She strode down the walk to the two-person buggy waiting at the street's edge.

I stared after her. *While I can?* Orpha was old, it was true, and increasingly frail. Was she on her final decline? I prayed not, even though I knew it would come one day soon. I wasn't ready to let her go, this wise, funny woman who knew me to my core, who had delivered me twenty-seven years ago.

Alma appeared in the doorway. "Come in, Rose, please. Nana's eager to see you." She stepped back so I could enter.

"Is she . . . ?" I couldn't finish.

"She's, well, you know her. But she's getting weaker."

I followed the dressmaker, a few years older than I, not into the parlor where Orpha usually spent her days reading in a rocking chair, but into the old lady's bedroom. She reclined in the bed, supported by pillows, and snored lightly.

I whispered to Alma, "I can come back another time."

"No." Alma also spoke softly. "She wanted to see you. Nana," she added, raising her voice. "Rose is here."

Orpha's eyes flew open. "There you are, my dear. I knew you would arrive. Come sit with an old lady."

Alma slipped out as I perched in the chair by the bed and took Orpha's soft hand. Her paper-fine skin was nearly translucent, with ropy veins rising up on the back of her hand.

"How did thee know I would come today?" I asked.

She smiled. "I know these things. And I know you have news for me."

"They're electrifying the trolley. Can you imagine? And the town is full of foreigners and people from all over the continent."

"For the Spring Opening." She nodded. "But I meant your own news, Rose. I sensed it, you know."

Tears sprang up. Orpha was the most remarkable woman I had ever met. I swiped at my eyes.

"It's true." I slid my other hand over my belly. "I am with child. Orpha, we're both so happy." David and I had been married last Ninth Month and had decided to let a family happen as it would.

"I'd say you're four months gone. Perhaps a little more?"

I bobbed my head. It hadn't taken long to conceive our first child.

"I've known all along but waited for you to tell me," she murmured.

"I pray I haven't hurt thy feelings by keeping it to myself."

"I'm not so easily wounded. Women tell in their own good time. Soon enough your dress will reveal your condition." She laughed. She'd always had a surprisingly hearty guffaw. It was now diminished in volume but not enthusiasm.

"I know." My plain dress was increasingly tight in the waist and across the bosom. "I've not had the morning nausea many women experience and only a few food aversions, so I've been eating with a great appetite."

"Good. Eating heartily will lead to a healthy newborn, as you well know."

"I do." I always told my clients the same thing. "Before I leave here, I plan to ask Alma to make me a couple of Aesthetic-style dresses to wear during the rest of my pregnancy."

"Tell her to use a light fabric. You'll be due in the heat of summer." Orpha tilted her head. "And your apprentice, Miss Beaumont, will watch over you?"

"Of course. Annie is ready to set out on her own. She's a fine midwife, Orpha. Truly. I plan to ask her to be my partner."

We sat holding hands in silence for a moment. Her eyes drifted shut.

With a little jerk, she opened them again. "I don't think I'm long for this world, my dear."

"Nonsense." I squeezed her hand, but gently. "I'm sure thee is wrong."

"No. In the same way I sensed your pregnancy, I sense death encroaching within me. You mustn't grieve. I've had a long and full life. I have a family who cares for me. I've safely brought hundreds of babies into this world. And I trained you and have watched you come into the full blossom of your profession, to which you were deeply called, and now your own family. My work is done."

My throat thickened. "But I want you to meet my baby." I very much did.

She laughed again. "I can guarantee I will not be alive in five months' time. Instead I'll be reunited with my Hiram and with all my loved ones who crossed the dark river ahead of me."

I gazed at her. "I was hoping for your prayers during my own labor. I've seen women through so much. What if my first baby is one of the difficult ones?"

She tilted her head. "Come closer with that belly of yours."

I scooted nearer. She reached out, laying both hands below my waist. When I'd taken her hand earlier, it had been cool compared to mine. Now warmth radiated from her touch. It went through my dress and deep inside me.

She moved her lips silently, then nodded. "All will be well. We've had a little talk, your babe and I. Don't you worry. The wee one will emerge in due time with no injury to either of you."

As odd as her prediction sounded, I had to believe her.

"And after this comes to pass, I shall watch over you both from the afterlife." When she straightened in the bed, the movement made her grimace. "Now run along, my dear Rose. I must rest again."

I bent over and kissed her forehead after her eyes closed. "Thee knows how much I love thee."

A smile spread across her face. She'd heard me, and that was all that mattered.

TWO

I PULLED MY CLOAK CLOSE ABOUT ME as I walked toward home—my new home, which I shared with my beloved husband. The most direct route to the lovely abode David had had custom-built for us last summer would not take me into the heart of town but instead past the Friends Meetinghouse where I worshipped weekly. But the annual showing of the carriage industry filled the town with so much excitement, I wanted to catch a glimpse of the happenings. I headed first toward the center.

Amesbury was world-famous for our graceful and well-built carriages. Once a year the carriage factories opened their doors to customers, who came from as far away as Australia. Residents opened their homes to the visitors, too, and every evening the Board of Trade hosted a dinner or an event, culminating with a gala at the end of the week. The industry's open house was called the Spring Opening, even though it was held at the end of winter. The weather didn't feel a bit spring-like today now the sun was going down.

My heart wasn't light and sunny, either. Would today be the last time Orpha would be able to speak to me? She was nearly eighty-five and had already survived an attack of apoplexy almost two years ago. She'd said she now felt death encroaching, and she seemed at peace about it. But I wasn't. I would miss her terribly.

I took in a breath and let it out. I could do nothing to keep her alive. My only course of action would be to stop by every day and offer my presence. And pray, after the manner of Friends, that her passage be a smooth and painless one. I took a moment to lean against a tree, close my eyes, and hold Orpha in God's Light before resuming my walk.

I slowed as I neared the opera house on Friend Street. Near the Armory, the tall ornate building was ablaze with lights and activity. It must be the site of tonight's event. It was across the street from here that we, a hundred women strong, had held placards in protest during the last presidential election. Women still didn't have the vote, but the effort to secure it was ongoing.

A man walking with a well-dressed couple approached on the sidewalk. "Good afternoon, Miss Carroll, I mean, Mrs. Dodge." Ned Bailey beamed from under his bowler.

A distant cousin of my brother-in-law, Ned had tried in vain to court me a couple of years ago. He was not to my liking, and I'd already fallen in love with David. But Ned was harmless and a good soul. As he was part of the family of the prosperous Bailey carriage manufacturers, he was nearly royalty in Amesbury.

"Hello, Ned," I said. "Thee must be deeply involved in this week's festivities."

"Indeed I am. May I present Mr. Justice Harrington and his wife, Luthera? They are visiting from the capital of our neighbor to the north, and I've been showing them around. Mr. and Mrs. Harrington, this is our town's esteemed midwife, Mrs. Rose Dodge."

We exchanged smiles and greetings, although I detected a barely concealed lip curl from Luthera when she heard the word "midwife." She was tall for a woman, standing perhaps two inches beyond my own five foot seven, with Justice yet a little taller.

"I've been to Montreal but not yet to Ottawa," I said. "I hear it's a lovely city."

"Yes, it is," Justice said. "We are the nation's capital and have much fine architecture as well as our famous Rideau Canal." His face was clean-shaven, and deep brown eyes sparkled under dark eyebrows. "Our own carriage industry is booming, so your Spring Opening presents a splendid opportunity to make connections. Isn't that right, Mrs. Harrington?"

"Yes." Her porcelain skin and flaxen hair were a contrast to the darker good looks of her husband. "It's my father's company, Montgomery Carriages, in which Mr. Harrington is taking an active role. We make the best carriages in all Canada." It was a good thing her maroon velvet toque was well secured on the side of her head. The way she lifted her chin the lace-trimmed topper might otherwise have slid off.

Ned clapped his hands. "Very good, very good. Well, we're off to call on my uncle before tonight's dinner." He beamed.

"I'm happy to have met thee, Luthera, and thee, Justice," I said. "I hope the week is satisfactory and enjoyable."

Luthera only nodded, her gloved hands clasped in front of her wool coat, which was cut in smooth lines with a diagonal overlap. The color matched her velvet hat.

Justice smiled. "We're thrilled to have a chance to meet Mr. Bailey, senior. Everyone in the industry admires the company's vehicles. Good day, Mrs. Dodge." He tipped his black stiff-fur hat and let Ned sweep them away.

They were an odd couple. Luthera seemed downright icy, while her husband was genial and projected an excitement about life itself. Well, one never knew what went on within a marriage. One's differences might feed the other's needs.

A drop-front phaeton passed by, followed by a runabout, a Bailey whalebone road wagon, and a fringed surrey filled with gaily clad young ladies. I reversed direction and headed for home. I'd seen enough of the happenings for today. The visitors and carriages would be around all week. I looked forward to nothing more than a quiet evening with my David.

THREE

I WAS FIXING COFFEE EARLY THE NEXT MORNING when I heard the clatter of the milk wagon. I pulled my dressing gown closer around me and stepped onto the side porch.

"'Morning, Mrs. Dodge." The milkman, the son of a local dairy farmer, set down the wire carrier holding two bottles and a pound of butter. He handed me the newspaper and picked up the empties. We'd prevailed on him to obtain the *Amesbury Daily News* for us as he passed through town every morning.

"Thank you, Sven."

"There's news about town." He shook his head, looking worried. "Not sure if it made the paper. A man was murdered in the night. One of them visitors."

No. "Murdered?" I brought my hand to my mouth. To my knowledge, Amesbury hadn't seen a murder since last summer, when a matron had been killed in her bed. My friend Bertie had been suspected in the crime, and I'd worked hard to untangle the facts and clear her name.

"Yes, ma'am."

"Does thee know the victim's name?"

"No, ma'am. I heard he was from up Canada way, though." He touched his white cap. "I'll see you on Thursday. Only milk?"

"Yes, thank thee." With the household being solely David and me for the time being, we didn't need more than thrice weekly deliveries. I brought the carrier and the paper inside.

David came downstairs a few minutes later, dressed except for his tie, and kissed my forehead as I perused the paper at the table. His hair was damp, and he smelled of soap. He'd made sure all the most modern conveniences were incorporated into our home, including indoor plumbing and a gas stove.

"Is this for the coffee?" He pointed to the pot of water on the stove, from which steam rose.

"Oh, dear! I forgot about it." I stood. "I'm sorry, darling. The milkman brought the most dreadful news." I hurried over to the pretty enameled double pot, white painted with pale blue flowers, which we'd

8

received as a wedding gift from David's father. He'd said it was imported from France and was the best way to brew coffee.

"I'll make the brew." David took the pot of water from me. "You sit down and tell me what transpired. Did a cow die?"

I plopped back in the chair and held up the paper. "Much worse. A Canadian man, here for the Spring Opening, was murdered sometime in the night. David, he's a gentleman Ned Bailey introduced me to only yesterday."

"You don't say." He dumped the coffee from the grinder's drawer into the top of the biggin, then slowly poured the boiled water over it.

"It's true." The paper didn't have much. A headline screamed, "Murder Taints Opening!" and a paragraph said only that Justice Harrington of Ottawa never returned to his rooms, according to his wife. A night watchman found his body in the alley behind the opera house, with gunshot wounds in his back. It said that, at the time the paper went to press, Acting Police Chief Kevin Donovan had no more information to offer.

"Goodness," I said. "This says our Kevin is acting chief of police. I wonder when his promotion happened."

"Didn't Chief Talbot come down with tuberculosis?" David asked. "I think I heard about his illness somewhere." He sat across from me. The coffee drip-dripped through its two filters.

"I don't know. If so, perhaps he went off to Saranac for the cure. There's a new sanitarium there. Or maybe he even traveled out to Colorado." I sniffed the rich aroma of the brew. Whoever discovered coffee was due an enormous medal in heaven. "I met a lady doctor yesterday who specializes in treating consumption."

"Dr. Chatigny? She's a fine physician. Where did you meet her?"

"She's caring for Orpha. I told thee she's failing. And Mary's mother made her promise to care for her old friend."

"Your mentor is in good hands, then. And the police department will similarly be in good hands with Detective Donovan, I daresay." David brought us each a cup of coffee.

I splashed milk into mine. "I would agree."

"Tell me more about this unfortunate Canadian."

Right. Last evening I hadn't mentioned my encounter with the Harringtons and Ned. I relayed to David how I'd met them on the street.

9

"Luthera and Justice are interesting names, are they not?" he asked.

"Indeed. And Ned was full of pride, being their escort about town. They were off to visit his uncle." I sipped the coffee and frowned. "Luthera seemed highly involved in her father's carriage company in Ottawa. And they were an odd couple. She nearly sneered at my being a midwife and acted quite cold, while he was friendly and full of life."

"A life cut short," David said. "Shot in the back, no less. A cowardly act if there ever was one. Who in the world would have wanted him dead?"

"That's the question, isn't it?" The clock in the next room donged seven soft chimes. I stood. "I will make thy breakfast, husband. Thee needs to be at the hospital by eight thirty for rounds, as it is Third Day, am I right?"

"Yes, my dear wife. What is your plan for the day?"

"I have several ladies in various stages of pregnancy coming this morning, and I'll pay a visit on the lovely Esther Ayensu this afternoon. She's due in two weeks' time. You know I like to make a home visit well in advance of the birth to make sure all is ready."

"She's the Negro lady you met after the Independence Day murder."

"Yes."

"You won't overexert yourself, will you?" He grabbed my hand and gently pulled me to him, resting his cheek on my belly.

I stood there for a moment, my hand on his shoulder, savoring the feeling of being loved. There was no man alive I'd rather create a family with than this one. I tapped the top of his head.

"This breakfast isn't going to cook itself, Dr. Dodge."

He chuckled and sat up straight. "Have I told you I loved you lately, Rose Carroll Dodge?"

FOUR

MY MORNING VISITORS SEEKING ANTENATAL CARE had been all abuzz with the news of the murder as well as the Spring Opening events. I'd had to steer each of them back to the reason they'd come, checking their baby's health and their own. Two were doing well, but one young bride, who had asked if she could barter fresh eggs for her fee, had not gained sufficient weight for her sixth month of pregnancy. I gave her back her basket of eggs and gently encouraged her to eat them, herself.

"We'll arrange something else after the birth, shall we?" I smiled as I sent her on her way, but I made a note in her chart. I would arrange for an anonymously delivered box of food every week. I hated to see impoverished women go hungry during a time when they needed to be eating more, not less.

The morning post had brought a note from Kevin asking me to stop by the police station this afternoon. After I supped on a simple midday meal of bread and ham as well as a sliced apple and a glass of milk, I mounted my bicycle. I'd go see the detective after I paid my visit to Esther. I pedaled along Whittier Street. I hadn't ridden much this winter because of the snow and ice, but today was milder than yesterday, and no hazardous ice remained. David worried a little about my bicycling while pregnant. I assured him it was not dangerous to the growing foetus, although I would certainly cease riding about when my belly grew unwieldy.

I coasted halfway down Carpenter Street to the tidy cottage the couple shared. Even though it was coincidence that Esther's husband, the carpenter Akwasi, had his home and shop on this street, it was aptly named.

Esther welcomed me in and offered me tea in a tidy and cheerful kitchen, with yellow curtains at the windows and an orange-and-red braided rug on the wide pine floor. I thanked her and sat at the table, which was covered with small cards and several pens and bottles of ink. Several of the cards had beautiful lettering on them. She slid them to the other side of the table.

"Is thee a calligrapher?" I asked. When I'd first met her, she worked stitching upholstery for the carriage industry.

She turned toward me from the stove, moving with the waddle of a woman near her term. "Yes. The Board of Trade hired me to make signs and place cards for the various Spring Opening events."

"Thee is very talented."

"Thank you. It's an occupation I can do from home." She smiled down at her large taut belly and smoothed her dress over it. She was a beautiful woman, as tall as I was, with large eyes, dark curly lashes, and skin the color of melted chocolate with plenty of cream mixed in. Her cheeks glowed with the fullness of her condition.

"That will be good after thy baby arrives."

"I've been getting more and more inquiries from businesses wanting placards and advertisements lettered, even some private invitations." She brought a teapot to the table. "This'll need to steep a bit."

"Where did thee learn to letter so beautifully?"

"I've always been drawing, and I started copying nice lettering last year. Using good-quality pens with different-sized nibs helps, too."

I gazed at the cards. "It looks completely professional. Well done."

"Thank you." Esther frowned a little. "Rose, I heard a Mr. Harrington was murdered in the night. Will you be involved in the investigation, as you were before?"

"I doubt it." Which might not be strictly true. I had dug into the case when her husband was falsely accused a couple of years earlier, and I planned to proceed directly to the police station after I left here. "I did meet the poor victim yesterday afternoon."

"I encountered him and his wife, as well, when I was delivering a batch of cards yesterday morning. They were talking to a carriage factory owner. William Parry, a rather unpleasant fellow." She poured out two cups of tea.

"He is a little unpleasant, although he has also suffered tragedy in his life."

"Mr. Ned Bailey introduced me to the Harringtons as I was leaving the opera house." She frowned. "Mr. Parry seemed to be having some kind of disagreement with Mr. Harrington."

"I'm not surprised."

"I pray the police don't come after my husband with more false charges this time," Esther said.

"I'm sure they won't. Has he any connection with the carriage industry?"

"No, not directly." She grimaced and let out a soft groan.

"A tightening? A cramp?" I asked.

"Yes. I've been having them more frequently."

"But they don't last long, am I correct, nor occur regularly?"

"Right, on both counts."

"It's thy body's way of preparing the womb for the real event," I said. "A kind of rehearsal of the contractions to come. Thee can also practice calming thyself and taking slow deep breaths when these pains occur. Such breathing is good preparation for the birth."

"Very well. See, it's now over." She sipped her tea. "Can I tell you something strange that's been happening?"

"Of course." I hoped it wasn't any kind of scurrilous vandalism because of the color of the couple's skin.

"I've been having the oddest dreams. They are very nearly nightmares."

"Oh?"

"Yes. Last night I dreamed I gave birth to a frog. And it seemed perfectly normal to do so. The night before our baby was a full-grown three-year-old, even though I knew I'd given birth the day before." She wrinkled her nose. "Akwasi was holding him like a newborn and rocking him, despite the child wearing short pants and shoes. Is there something wrong with me?"

I laughed and patted her hand. "Esther, this is perfectly normal. I would think it odd if thee weren't having such dreams. Most pregnant ladies do as they near their time, especially first-time mothers. Your actual fears might be different ones, but this is the way your mind works it out while you sleep. Please don't let these dreams disturb you."

"All right. But I do have fears, you see. I'm worried I won't be able to give birth easily. It's my first, and how will I know what to do? What if something goes wrong?"

"I will be with thee, I and my assistant. Thee has met Annie Beaumont. She's very good. We shall guide thee through." I took a sip of tea.

"I feel silly worrying. My mother was a slave. She birthed seven babies with barely any help at all. I was born only three years after Emancipation."

"Such a life must have been horrific and painful for her."

Akwasi Ayensu had been an escaped slave when our town's—and our Meeting's—abolitionist poet, John Whittier, sheltered him and helped him get an education and be trained in a trade. Akwasi frequently attended Friends Meeting for Worship and had brought Esther several times. It was inconceivable to me that humans had thought they could own another human, but our country had a long, dark, and sordid history of exactly that.

"Mama—her name was Glory—was a strong woman with deeply held values," Esther went on. "She did what she had to to stay alive and keep us safe."

"Of course she did. Thee is strong, too. I have every confidence in thy abilities and the ability of thy body to do what women have been doing for millennia." I stood. "Now, why doesn't thee show me the bedroom and thy supplies? We'll do an examination, and I'll let thee know how much longer I think thee has before the baby comes."

FIVE

"THEE IS THE CHIEF OF POLICE NOW, KEVIN," I said after he showed me into his office. "I congratulate thee."

"Acting chief." He plopped into a creaky chair behind the desk in his own office, not the chief's, and the desk was its usual mess of papers and books. He ran a hand over his round head, mussing the short-cropped red hair. "Frankly, it's a thankless job, but I suppose I should thank you, Miss Rose."

I suppressed a smile. I'd never been successful at convincing him to leave off the title and simply call me Rose. And he hadn't changed my moniker after I'd become a Mrs. I was fond of the detective and didn't mind a bit.

He went on. "And now we have a murder during the Spring Opening. Things couldn't get much worse."

"I'm sorry. It must be a thankless job. David thought perhaps Norman Talbot had contracted tuberculosis."

"Yes, more's the pity. He took himself off to some wretched place in the Adirondack Mountains of New York State to attempt a cure. You know, sitting out on balconies in the sunshine, drinking clean water, breathing fresh air, those kinds of boring things."

Saranac Lake. The sanitarium opened by Edward Trudeau, the scientist who had first isolated and cultured the tuberculosis bacterium only half a decade ago.

"How did the chief contract the disease?" I asked. "It's often those who live in desperate and crowded circumstances who fall ill. Norman must reside in decent housing and so forth."

"He does. Talbot's a gruff, rather officious man, but in fact he has a big heart. He was taking food and games to the young boys down at the Flats. Doing his Christian charity. He must have caught it from one of them." Kevin cleared his throat. "But about the murder of poor Mr. Harrington."

"I read he was shot in the back."

"Yes, several times. Some coward killed him. We haven't found the weapon, in case you were about to ask."

15

I had been, but I moved on. I relayed how Ned had introduced me to the couple. "He said they were off to meet Mr. Bailey, senior, Ned's uncle."

"And apparently they did, then moved on to the banquet in the opera house."

"Does thee have thoughts about who might have done the deed, and why?"

"In truth, I don't, Miss Rose. Mrs. Harrington is understandably distraught. At the same time, she's clearheaded enough to be demanding an arrest."

"I suppose it could have been some malingerer who thought he could rob a rich Canadian."

"That's possible." He made a little grunt. "The Titans of Industry, as they call themselves, came here in force to tighten the screws on me."

The self-named titans were the owners of the better-known carriage factories, as well as Cyrus Hamilton of the Hamilton Mills Company. "Was William Parry among them?" I asked.

"Yes."

"I just came from a pregnant lady who said she witnessed William arguing with Justice Harrington yesterday morning."

"Oh? Her name, if you would be so kind." Kevin put a stubby pencil to paper and gazed at me.

"Hmm." I tilted my head and gazed back at him. "Does thee remember the case of Akwasi Ayensu two years ago?"

"Yes." Kevin wrinkled his nose. "I was sorely mistaken about the culprit."

Yes, thee was. "He's now married to Esther, a calligrapher producing signage for the Spring Opening. It was she who overheard the disagreement."

"Think she'd talk to me?"

"I'm not sure. She's due to give birth very soon, likely within the next week or two."

He let out a miserable sigh.

"But I'll ask her if she's willing," I said. "Or to speak on the telephone, perhaps."

"I would greatly appreciate you doing so, Miss Rose. Also keep your ears open for talk of some kind of plans. The elder Mr. Bailey claims papers of his have gone missing."

"What kind of plans?"

"For a new carriage design, he said. To tell the truth, I'm not sure he's all there upstairs." Kevin tapped the side of his head with a finger. "If you get my meaning."

"I will listen for such talk." But the patriarch of the legendary Bailey family going dotty? That would be a shame.

The clock on the wall ticked over to two o'clock. "Oh, Jesus and . . ." He clapped his hand over his mouth. "Forgive me, Miss Rose. It's just that I have a meeting at Town Hall I'm about to be late for."

I laughed. "I wish thee luck. I will help in any way I can, thee knows."

"I do know, and I thank you."

"I'm sorry I neglected to ask about thy family."

"They are well, thanks be to the saints. My wife always loves your visits." He stood and grabbed his hat.

"I'll try to go see her soon, and the children." I rose. "And Kevin? Good luck."

SIX

I STOOD WITH MY BICYCLE ON THE WALK outside the police station, undecided as to my direction. I could ride home, put my feet up, and have a quiet afternoon. I could pick up a few items at the Mercantile, pay a visit to my niece Faith in the newspaper office where she now worked as a reporter, or stop by Mary Chatigny's office to ask her more details about Orpha's health. Or all of it. We still had a plentiful amount of a hearty beef stew David had concocted on First Day, so I didn't need to worry about preparing dinner.

My husband insisted he found cooking relaxing, and he'd developed quite the talent for it. On days when he wasn't overly busy with his responsibilities as a physician, he often prepared a big pot of something that we could dine on for more than one meal. I loved that he was willing to share the domestic chores. I'd hired the sister of the kitchen girl in my former home to come in mornings to clean the kitchen and the house so neither David nor I had to take time away from our work. We also sent out the laundry every week. We both knew once the baby arrived, I would be busy nursing him—or her—and David had insisted we could well afford to hire out cleaning and laundry.

For now, I resolved to first visit Mary's office on Elm Street. I'd noted the address in an advertisement for her services in this morning's newspaper. I walked my bicycle down Main Street toward Market Square, passing Nayson Druggist, John F. Johnson Books and Stationery, and the Wendall Barber Shop, among other establishments. The road was too lively with carriages of all sorts pulled by horses in all hues for me to ride alongside. The rushing Powow River flowed under Main Street at one point, and then partly through more Hamilton Mill buildings, providing power as it descended to the lower millyard. I made my way past the square and the busy railroad depot, then pushed the bike up Elm toward Carriage Hill.

When I was nearly to the address, a woman approached on the walk. I took a second look as she drew closer. Yes, it was Marie Deorocki, an Amesbury lady I'd met on Cape Cod last fall.

"Good afternoon, Marie." I slowed and smiled at her.

"Rose, hello." She was thinner than she had been half a year earlier, and her woolen coat was buttoned right up despite today's milder temperatures and sunshine. She turned her face away and coughed into a handkerchief. "Pardon me."

"Is thee unwell?"

"I admit to not feeling as well as I might, yes." A faint crackling rale came from her chest as she breathed.

"I hope thee recovers soon. It was good to see thee."

"And likewise, you, Rose." She bobbed her head and continued down the road.

I found the large new house on the corner of Marston Street. It featured a hip roof, ornate trim, a bow window on the front, and a glassed-in front entryway. A discreet sign reading *Dr. M. Chatigny* hung outside a side door. Mary herself opened it after I rang the bell for the office.

"Mrs. Dodge." Her pale eyebrows went up. "Did you come about Mrs. Perkins?"

"No. Well, in a way. I don't want to disturb your business, but I wondered if you have a moment to talk."

She glanced to her side at a clock hanging on the wall. "My next patient is not due to arrive until three o'clock. Do come in." She showed me into an office with a large desk under a tall window, a comfortable armchair, and an examining table. A small sink was attached to the wall near the table. "Please sit." She sank onto the swivel chair at the desk and turned to face me.

"I thank thee," I said. "Does thee bear the brunt of disagreeable treatment for being a lady doctor? I shouldn't think there are many of both thy sex and training."

"Good heavens, there are not. We are few and had to fight every step of the way to get as far as we have. It's the plight of women everywhere, isn't it?"

"Certainly, any who wish to do work normally carried out by the male of the species," I agreed.

"And yes, I have had quite my share of unpleasantness from those who feel threatened by me. I don't care. I stand on my reputation, and my husband has always supported my efforts."

I gazed at a poster hanging on the wall, which displayed an

intricate drawing of the human respiratory system. "Does thee have a high number of tuberculosis patients?"

"Yes. I'm afraid the number is ever rising, and we have no treatment to speak of. Are you yourself feeling ill, Mrs. Dodge?"

"No, not at all. But I did want to talk about Orpha, if thee will. When I visited her yesterday, she told me she senses death approaching within her. Does she have a cancer of some kind?"

"I don't believe so. As I think I mentioned, what she has is advanced age. All the body's systems begin to break down with time. She has already lived more than eight decades, which is remarkable. The apoplexy weakened her even though she survived it. You might know better than I what an intuitive being she is. I'm not surprised she understands she is dying."

I only nodded. I truly wasn't surprised, either. A bell clanged outside but slowly, not furiously as it would if it signaled fire. The doctor and I both glanced out the window to see a fire wagon followed by a procession of decorated carriages drive toward the town center.

She made a tsking sound. "I daresay Amesbury will see an uptick in tuberculosis in the coming month. So many strangers are here bringing their germs from all over the world."

"I hadn't thought of that aspect of the Spring Opening."

"We now know the disease can be spread from person to person, via spittle or coughing, among other avenues. I understand the local commerce needs the sales, but medically it's a pity."

"And if the visitors associate closely with a resident who is sick, they might carry the illness home with them," I said.

"Exactly. With neither a vaccine nor a cure available, it truly is a grim prospect. I've heard rumblings from Germany that Dr. Koch is developing a cure, but I imagine it will come to naught. Much of the populace is unfortunately opposed to the use of any vaccine. Even when one is developed, it won't be easy to convince the common person of its necessity."

The clock now read five before three. I stood and extended my hand. "I thank thee for thy time, Mary. I plan to stop in at Orpha's before I return home this afternoon."

She rose and shook my hand. "If Mrs. Perkins shows a marked change, please have her granddaughter telephone me."

I nodded. "I'll let myself out." I closed the door behind me and heard a cough from farther down the side street. It was William Parry trudging up the hill that Marston ended in. I hadn't seen the carriage factory owner since the murders two years ago, when he'd lost nearly his whole family. His factory, rebuilt after the Great Fire of 1888, sat along Oakland Street not far from here. I waited for William to arrive, then greeted him.

"Miss Carroll." His cheeks above his chinstrap beard were flushed with the exertion. He didn't look happy to see me.

"It's actually Mrs. Dodge now. How fares little Billy?" I wondered why the factory owner hadn't arrived in a Parry carriage, but I didn't ask.

He brightened, beaming. "He's a healthy strapping lad of nearly two, as you know."

I did know, having delivered the boy. "I'm happy to hear it. How is the Opening going for thee and thy factory?"

"We're having an excellent showing." He scowled. "But the matter of that Canadian being murdered is casting a shadow on the whole affair."

"I should think it might." I was not surprised that William went straight to business rather than expressing sorrow at the tragedy or sympathy for the widow. I'd always found him a self-centered type of man. "Had thee done business with the Harringtons' firm?"

"We were about to sign a deal, as a matter of fact. Now I don't know what will happen, more's the pity."

A deal? I wondered what kind. "When I met them yesterday, it appeared that Luthera holds as much power in the company as her husband did."

"Be that as it may." He cleared his throat. "If you will excuse me, I, uh, have a consultation to attend." He glanced behind me at Mary's office.

"Good day, then." I stepped aside and retrieved my cycle. Did he have consumption, too? He'd looked as hale and well fed as he had two years ago. Well, it wasn't my business. And he was certainly in good hands with Mary Chatigny.

SEVEN

"GOOD AFTERNOON, ROSE." Store manager Catherine Toomey greeted me from behind the counter at the Mercantile. Besides being manager of the busy shop, she was a rosy-cheeked, friendly mother of three and the grandmother of a little boy I had helped into the world.

I waved and made my way to the notions area. I'd run out of black thread and needed to reattach a button on one of David's coats. The store, which sold all manner of dry goods, also stocked hardware, paints, toiletries, tonics, and staples like flour and sugar.

From behind a row of shelving, I heard coughing. I hoped it wasn't someone with tuberculosis. The ill should be home resting, not out making purchases in public, or worse, working at an establishment and possibly transmitting the bacteria to those shopping.

I added a new box of writing paper to my basket, since I was running low, and a supply of pencils for my bookkeeping. As I passed through a small section of children's toys, I fingered a carved baby rattle. I scolded myself silently, setting it down. Our infant wouldn't need a rattle until well into the fall, and I didn't want to tempt fate by acquiring toys for him — or her — until after the birth.

Marie stood at the counter when I arrived with my basket.

"We meet again, Marie." I smiled at her.

"You two know each other?" Catherine asked.

"I met Rose when I was caring for my mother in West Falmouth in September," Marie told the shopkeeper.

"Excellent. Here are your tonics." Catherine handed her several bottles wrapped in brown paper. "Now, do read the dosages, Mrs. Deorocki. These aren't to be trifled with."

As she nodded, I again heard the ominous crackle of the rale.

Marie paid, said goodbye, and walked toward the exit, coughing anew before the door shut behind her.

"She's not well," I said in a soft tone, even though no one else seemed to be nearby.

Catherine surveyed the store and lowered her voice, too. "No, she's not."

"I met her on Elm Street a little while ago as I was going to visit with Dr. Mary Chatigny. Does Marie have—"

"Galloping consumption? She does. We volunteer at the same Catholic charity and have become good friends."

"She should be resting."

"Aye, she should. I tell her as much, and so does her husband. She says she has too much to do. I'm afraid she'll collapse one of these days, and then what will she be able to accomplish?" Catherine set my purchases on the counter and began to tally up the prices.

"How are thy twins, and little Charlie?" I asked.

"Charlie's a right sturdy lad, and fearless, even though he can't see a speck."

A disease transmitted from his mother's birth passage had blinded the boy after he'd entered the world. I'd asked my sightless friend Jeanette to assist the parents in understanding how to cope, educate their son, and help him navigate the world.

Catherine beamed. "My girlies have been helping to take care of him. Funny, he's their nephew despite them being only six and him a toddler. Now, what else can I get you today?"

"Nothing, I think." I peered at the glass-fronted cabinet behind her, which was full of bottles, pills, and powders. "What kind of tonics did Marie buy, may I ask?"

"Mellin's Emulsion and Dr. Sproule's tonic, two of our strongest, as well as Dr. Ayer's Cherry Pectoral Plaster and Beecham's Pills. She thinks they'll cure her. That and prayer."

"Prayer can be powerful," I offered.

"I suppose. Say, what do you think about that Canuck gent being murdered?" Her eyebrows went up.

"I think it's a sad and horrible end to a young man's life, no matter where he was from."

She crossed herself. "Will you be working with the police again?" Catherine's witness testimony had helped solve a case a year ago.

"I'll be poking around as I can. Naturally, the department will be doing the actual investigation."

"Tell them they ought to . . ." Catherine glanced around the store again, but we were still alone. She spoke in a near whisper. "They might want to look into the wife. Those two were in here yesterday. I overheard her berating the poor fellow. They were behind the paint shelves, and I'm sure she thought I couldn't hear." The shopkeeper laughed heartily. "My sainted husband says I have better ears than a dog's."

"Interesting. I shall pass that along." I smiled. "About Luthera Harrington, not about thy acute hearing."

"That's fine, then." She looked me up and down. "You're with child, are you now, Rose?"

"I am." My cheeks heated up. "I feel quite blessed about it. But thee could tell? I didn't think my condition was that obvious yet."

She gave a knowing nod, with a finger next to her eye. "I've borne three, and you and I both helped my daughter-in-law birth little Charlie. But it's also that I watch people in here all day long. You've the look, Rose, and there's no mistaking it. Your garment is a bit snug, too."

"Thee has a keen eye as well as keen ears. I'm ordering new dresses from a seamstress to accommodate my growing girth." I paid her for my purchases and bade her farewell. As I walked up Friend Street, I mused on what she'd said before we started discussing my pregnancy. Would Luthera have been so bold as to shoot her own husband here in a strange town? Perhaps she thought few would know her, and she'd be able to get away with the crime. But why?

EIGHT

"ROSE, WHAT A SURPRISE," my niece Faith said at the door to the busy newsroom of the *Amesbury Daily News* a few minutes later.

"I was passing by and thought I'd stop in. I've never visited thee in thy workplace before."

I glanced beyond her at a room full of desks at which sat men in shirtsleeves and vests, scribbling away or conversing. One leaned back in his chair chewing on a red pencil. The young fellow who had let me in and fetched Faith scurried busily about. When a reporter wearing a visor waved a paper in the air, the lad ran over, grabbed it, and took it into another room.

"Is thee the only female employed here?" I asked.

"Pretty much. There's a lady who types letters for the boss and makes the coffee, but no other reporters of my sex." She frowned, drawing her brows together over brown eyes so much like my own. "The editor keeps asking me to cover society events instead of the news. That's a girl's purview, he says."

"It's a start, isn't it? And thee is writing for a living, which is what thee has always wanted to do."

"I know, Rose. And I'm still young. But if they'd even let me cover the Board of Trade proceedings, that would be a start." She whispered, "The board is gathering in an hour to discuss the effect of the killing on the week's activities, and it's an open meeting. Do I get to cover it? I do not."

I patted her arm. "By and by thee will."

"But speaking of news—" Faith glanced over her shoulder. "Come into the hall with me."

We moved around the corner into the hallway where I'd come in.

"Is thee on the case of the Harrington murder?" she asked.

"I spoke with Kevin Donovan about it, but I haven't really learned anything of interest."

"Will thee tell me when thee does? If I could get a scoop, they might start taking me seriously around here."

I would hate to put her in danger by encouraging her to snoop around. On the other hand, she was nineteen, a married woman, and had brave ambitions. After all, I'd put myself in danger more than once in the pursuit of justice.

"I will," I agreed. "Kevin did mention that the senior Bailey reported some plans having gone missing. You might keep an ear out for information regarding those."

Her eyebrows went up. "There's been nothing in the newsroom about that. The Baileys must want to keep it quiet for now."

I nodded. "And here's something else thee can do. One of the reasons Kevin values my counsel on cases is because I can go places he never will be able to."

"Like women's bedrooms, for instance?"

"Precisely." I bobbed my head. "Go to the Spring Opening social events. Take notes on who acts suspicious, who talks to whom. Introduce thyself to the ladies. They all love having their names in the newspaper. Thee might overhear a newsworthy confidence or a tidbit thee can use."

Faith gave me an impulsive hug. "Rose, thee is brilliant."

I laughed. "Not by any stretch of the imagination. But I am a wee bit older than thee and somewhat more experienced in these matters." I sobered. "See if Luthera Harrington attends."

"Does thee suspect the wife?" she whispered.

"I don't know. By rights Luthera shouldn't be going out, as she presumably is in mourning. But she seems to be invested in her father's firm."

"Montgomery Carriage Company."

I bobbed my head. "Luthera might well attend," I said. "Has thee seen her?"

"No, I don't think so. Or if I did, I didn't know it was she."

"She has lovely pale skin like a creamy bleached linen and light hair the color of flax." I pushed my glasses back up the bridge of my nose. "When I met her yesterday, she was quite stylishly dressed. She should be easy to find. I'm sure all the ladies will be clustering around her offering their sympathies."

"And hoping to pick up pieces of gossip, I daresay. You know, Rose, I'll bet Nellie Bly never has to cover balls and teas."

"The intrepid lady reporter?"

"Yes." Faith's face gleamed. "Did thee hear she recently arrived back from her trip around the world?"

"I didn't. She circumnavigated the entire globe?"

"She did. She traveled alone and sent back reports all along the way. It was quite the feat."

"Mrs. Weed?" The fresh-faced runner popped his head around the corner, his voice cracking. "Boss wants to see ya."

"Thank thee," Faith said to him, but to me she rolled her eyes. "Maybe if I were Nellie Bly, I'd get some respect from my peers."

An amused snort slipped out of me. "Thee will be more respected even than her in time. Mark my words, Faith Bailey Weed."

NINE

ALMA SET DOWN A BOLT OF A SPRIGGED LAWN FABRIC she'd been showing me after I left the newsroom.

"I know this one is too colorful for a good Quaker. But it's quite lightweight for summer, Rose."

"It's pretty, I'll grant thee, but I shouldn't be wearing flowers," I said. "And the colors must be muted to conform with our custom of simple dress. Does thee have a lawn in a pale gray or green, perhaps?"

"I don't here, but I can order some in."

"Any plain color will do."

"I wish some of those fancy ladies liked simpler garments." Alma shook her head. "One of them was in this morning. She's a new widow and demanded I make her a black dress, but with puffy sleeves as well as the bodice shirring and slimmer skirt profile of this year's fashions."

Luthera. "Does she have skin like fine china and light hair?"

Alma scrunched up her nose. "How did you know?"

"I met Luthera Harrington yesterday. She's a new widow because her husband was murdered last night."

"Murdered?" Alma nearly screeched, then clapped her hand over her mouth, glancing downstairs toward Orpha's room.

"Alas, yes."

"I guess I didn't attend to the news today. Anyway, she said wanted the dress by tonight. I told her that wasn't possible, but that I had a new dress close to that style I made for a slender lady whose husband had died. Unfortunately, the lady passed, too, before she could pick up the garment. Mrs. Harrington was reluctant, but she had no alternative." She glanced at the clock. "I have two hours to finish the alterations."

Luthera must be determined to attend tonight's function. Which was unseemly for a widow, but at least she'd be dressed appropriately.

"May I visit with Orpha?" I asked.

"Always."

We moved through the quiet house. "Where are thy daughters?"

"My husband took them to stay with his parents in Kittery, Maine. Between my work and caring for Nana, I have my hands full, and Mr.

Latting was overdue for a visit, anyway. He'll be back on Sunday, but the girls will stay on another week."

"Is it thy father or thy mother who is Orpha's child? I would have thought he or she would want to be here during her last weeks." Or days. Especially a daughter might long to care for her aged mother as she passed from this world.

Alma cast her gaze upward. "It's my father who is her son. He's a rather difficult man, unfortunately. My mother loves Nana, and she would be here. But she obeys her husband, and he wants his wife by his side. If they still lived in Amesbury, I'm sure Mother would find ways to pop in. But they moved down to Ipswich after I married, and it's too hard for her to get away unnoticed."

Good heavens. "That's too bad."

"Yes, it is." She gave a quick laugh. "If my husband tried to keep me from doing what I wished? I would no longer be married."

"I'm glad to hear it." I thought it was a blessing Alma had not adopted her parents' ways in this regard.

Before we stepped into Orpha's room, Alma grabbed my hand, stopping me. "Rose, you see babies into the world. Will you be so kind as to see Orpha out? She mentioned to me it would give her great peace to be ushered into the next realm by her favorite midwife. You."

My throat thickened, but I swallowed down the emotion. "It would be an immense honor, Alma. Traditionally midwives have always assisted at both ends of life. I have a telephone at home." I could be a death midwife as well as a birthing one.

She nodded.

"I shall continue to stop by every day, but if her death seems imminent, please summon me."

"And it won't upset your condition?" She snuck a look at my waist.

"Of course not. This baby is safe inside for the duration. Thee should know, Alma. Thee has borne children. I'm not ill, I'm pregnant."

I followed her into the room. Alma was obviously keeping my mentor clean and comfortable, as the space blessedly did not smell of urine or worse.

"She's been sleeping most of the day," Alma said. "And she's barely eating, Rose. Wake her, if you can."

I blew out a breath, then leaned down and touched Orpha's soft cheek. Her lids drifted open.

"Rose. I'm glad you're here." She gave a faint smile. "Alma, dear, may I have some of that soup you offered me earlier? Perhaps Rose can help me sip it."

Alma bustled off. I picked up the hairbrush on the side table and began stroking Orpha's hair gently back away from her face. It wasn't completely white, having dark grizzled through, and the texture was soft while still a bit kinky. Orpha had told me long ago she'd had a Negro ancestor generations earlier, which was one reason she'd never turned away any pregnant woman from her care, no matter her skin color.

"That feels lovely," she murmured.

"Good." I dampened a cloth from a washbasin and wiped her face and hands. "There. Better?"

"I am much refreshed. Would you mind terribly handing me that small jar?" Her gaze shifted to a squat container on the bedside table. "My skin feels parched."

I opened the jar and held it for her to scoop out a couple of fingers of a white cream. I inhaled the scent as she gently rubbed it into her face.

"Calendula and lavender." I smiled at her. "This is why thee always smells lovely."

"Those herbs are healing, too." She finished and said, "Help me sit up a little, please."

I helped her, even though she winced at the effort. After Alma brought the soup, I stayed, feeding Orpha spoonfuls of a thick broth until she'd had enough.

"Did Alma tell you my request?" she asked, after I helped her get comfortable on her pillow.

"She did. Nothing would honor me more than being thy end-of-life midwife, dear Orpha."

"Good. That's settled, then." Her eyes closed.

I slipped out, calling a goodbye to Alma as I went. And wiping my eyes.

TEN

My PERAMBULATION HOME TOOK ME BY THE TOWN HALL as the church bells tolled five times. Faith had said the Board of Trade meeting was open to the public, and David wouldn't be home until six o'clock. I lifted my skirts and marched up the stairs. I might be able to learn something. I'd at least be able to report back to Faith on the proceedings.

I edged into the back of the hall. On a raised floor at the front sat an array of men. I spied the elder Bailey, mill owner Cyrus Hamilton, William Parry, and three other gentlemen. I thought one owned the highly successful hat factory down on the river. I peered at the man next to William and realized it was Jonathan Sherwood, the manager at the Lowell Boat Shop. I'd met him several times during previous investigations and had found him a quiet, intelligent, thoughtful man. The meeting hadn't started yet, and the board members conversed among themselves, although Mr. Bailey was nodding off.

The audience was made up of shopkeepers and the owners of the many smaller factories who supplied parts and upholstery for the carriage industry. Some women occupied seats, although men comprised the majority. I didn't know any of them well, but I'd delivered babies for a number of their wives. Ned Bailey sat in a row near the back. I slid into the wooden chair next to him. As I did, a mustachioed man seated behind him raised a dark eyebrow and gave me a rakish grin. His eyes were a startling green in a deeply tanned face.

I nodded at him and greeted Ned as I sat.

"Good evening, Mrs. Dodge. What brings you here?"

"Curiosity, mostly. I'm wondering how the murder of one of our visitors will affect the week's events."

"A tragedy, that death," he said with a somber look, then his expression brightened. "Do you know, even though commerce seems to be flourishing for carriages, I think the future lies in self-propelled vehicles. Motorcars."

"Is that so?" I asked. "What would propel them?"

"Why, a German put an electric motor in a carriage body only two years ago. It's called the Flocken Elektrowagen. And another Kraut named Benz added an internal combustion engine to a carriage before that. Imagine it. We could do away with horse-drawn carriages entirely." Ned's eyes gleamed.

I gazed at him. He'd always seemed a silly man to me. This looking forward was a new turn for Ned Bailey.

"Even here," I began, "the horse-drawn trolley is about to disappear in favor of the electrically powered one."

"I know. I'm thinking Amesbury would be perfect for the new industry. We already build the best carriage bodies. Let us add a source of power and sell them to the world!"

"Will thee start the first Amesbury motorcar company?"

"You've read my mind, Mrs. Dodge."

I remembered what Kevin had said earlier about the plans. "Ned, I heard a rumor about plans being stolen from thy uncle. Does thee know anything about that?"

He whipped his head toward me, his eyes narrowed. "Who did you hear that from?"

Maybe I shouldn't have mentioned what the detective told me. "Oh, around town."

"What kind of plans?" Ned asked.

"I don't know." That, at least, was the truth. Or . . . no—it wasn't. Kevin had said they were plans for a new design of carriage. I kept my mouth shut even as I wondered if they could be for a horseless carriage. I hoped Ned wasn't involved in the theft or, worse, responsible for it.

Ned drummed his fingers on his thigh as his heel jiggled up and down, making his leg jitter. I glanced away when my dear friend Bertie Winslow, Amesbury's postmistress, slid into the seat on the other side of me.

"Bertie, how lovely to see thee." I smiled at her.

"You know I like to keep my finger on the pulse of the town." Her hat, trimmed today with a purple ribbon, sat as always at a rakish angle on her curly blond hair. "Hello, there, Mr. Bailey," she said to Ned.

He nodded at her. "Miss Winslow."

She squeezed my hand and whispered, "Any news on the you know what?"

I assumed she referred to the murder. "Not yet."

At the front, Cyrus Hamilton rapped a gavel on the table in front of the board. "The public meeting of the Amesbury Board of Trade will come to order."

"Come for coffee in the morning?" I asked Bertie. "We can talk then." My new abode was down the street from where she lived with her sweetheart.

"You're on, Rosetta. Eight isn't too early?"

"Not at all."

Out of the corner of my eye I saw Kevin take a place on the opposite side of the hall, standing with his back to the wall. These mysterious plans had to be at the center of the mystery. Didn't they?

"The first matter of business tonight is the unfortunate turn of events of which I am sure you are all aware," Cyrus began.

I'd had some dealings with him two years ago when his son, who was sick in the head, committed a crime. Cyrus himself was a kind man who had shown great generosity to my brother-in-law.

"Mr. Sherwood?" Cyrus gestured toward Jonathan.

"In case any of you has been too busy to read the news today, it is this." Jonathan stood to speak. "Mr. Justice Harrington of Ottawa, Canada, and the Montgomery Carriage Company, was brutally murdered sometime during last night or the early hours of this morning."

A gasp went up from several in the audience who apparently had been otherwise occupied. Most of the rest nodded knowingly or in sorrow.

"Our excellent police force is now led by the able Mr. Donovan." Jonathan gestured toward Kevin, who tipped his hat. "The force is busy investigating." Jonathan picked up a piece of paper and read from it. "The Board of Trade has determined that the week's events shall go forward. At tonight's soiree we shall pay tribute to Mr. Harrington and lift a glass in his memory. We have every confidence that the streets of our fair town are safe, and that our visitors are not at risk. That said, it always behooves one to conduct one's affairs with all due caution."

A murmur rose up around me. I was sure people were wondering if perhaps we weren't entirely safe going about our business, traveling here and there, venturing forth after dark. In fact, a murderer was still at large.

Cyrus rapped the gavel on the table. "Order, please. The board will now move on to two other items of business. Thank you, Mr. Sherwood."

"I'm leaving, Bertie," I whispered. "See you in the morning."

"I'll be there," she murmured.

"Good day, Ned. And good luck with thy new venture."

"Thank you." He frowned. "Best be careful, Mrs. Dodge. All due caution and so forth."

"Have no fear. I shall." I knew, coming from him, that "be careful" wasn't a threat but instead a more caring admonition. I also knew I had many reasons to proceed with caution, a growing baby and a beloved husband being among the very top.

ELEVEN

I WAS READY FOR THE DAY when Bertie knocked on the back door at eight the next morning. She looked ready, too, in a crisp white shirtwaist, a gray striped skirt, and a stylish turquoise jacket with a matching turquoise ribbon in her plush black hat. Petite Bertie loved fashion.

"Where's that handsome husband of yours?" She sat at the kitchen table and drew out a wrapped packet.

"He left for Anna Jaques Hospital not ten minutes ago." I poured her a cup of coffee and sat with mine across from her.

"He should hang out his shingle here in Amesbury. That way, he wouldn't have to cross the mighty Merrimack River every day."

"I've gently suggested the same. David is considering it. He could affiliate himself with the Methodist Hospital on Market Street instead of the one in Newburyport."

"I would advise the move." Bertie unwrapped the packet. "Brought you some of Sophie's Portuguese sticky buns. They're quite delicious, and you're eating for two now."

"I am, and these look lovely." I brought plates and napkins to the table. "I thank thee."

"Sophie finds it relaxing to bake, and it provides a welcome break from her lawyering." She looked me up and down. "Rose, I daresay you're fuller of figure than you were yesterday. That baby is growing well in you."

I'd recently told my good friend the happy news, as well as my nieces and nephews. I now laughed and patted my midsection. "It is growing well, and I feel well, too. Only fuller, as thee says. My new dresses won't be finished a day too soon." Today I'd donned my roomiest garment, an older work dress, as I had no client visits this morning. Even it was snug. Still, I took a bite of a bun, and then another. It was never wise for a pregnant woman to skimp on food if it was available.

"Now, let's talk about the murder before I have to get myself off to the post office." Bertie's eyes sparkled. "What do you know?"

"Alas, almost nothing. Kevin told me something about plans for a new design going missing from the older Bailey's possession, but he offered no details about the nature of the plans except that they were for a carriage."

"Think the dead man might have made off with them and was killed for his misdeed?"

"Maybe. Before you came into the meeting yesterday, Ned Bailey told me he might be opening a motorcar factory. Apparently in Germany they are either adding electricity or some kind of engine to carriages so they can move under their own power."

"A horseless carriage. Just think of it, Rosetta. No more streets filled with manure, no more giving a boy a coin to watch your steed when you run into a store to do an errand. It would be a different world, wouldn't it?"

"It certainly would. But what Ned said made me wonder if somehow his plans were involved. When I said I'd heard something about missing plans, he inquired rather sharply and then acted nervous."

"What else do you know about the unfortunate Canadian?" she asked.

At another knock on the door, I went to it. "Faith, what a delight." I kissed her cheek.

"I wanted to tell thee about the soiree last night," she said, rosy-cheeked and breathless.

"Come in, my dear. Bertie and I are having coffee and discussing the murder."

"Of course you are. Why am I not surprised?" Faith laughed and greeted Bertie.

I brought her a cup of coffee and a plate. Faith was as slender as I, or as I had been before my present condition evidenced itself. She could easily consume a sweet baked treat even if she'd eaten breakfast twenty minutes earlier. She shed her coat and sat.

"Bertie had just asked about Justice Harrington," I said. "He worked for his father-in-law's company, Montgomery Carriages in Ottawa. That's about the extent of my knowledge. Was Luthera at the soiree, Faith?"

"Indeed she was, in a new black gown, looking tragic." She sipped the coffee. "But I had the feeling she was putting on an act. She certainly let the other ladies fuss over her, especially after Robert Clarke led a short tribute to her husband."

After I'd delivered the Clarkes' youngest child almost two years ago, I'd been able to save the mother, Georgia, from hemorrhaging. Her husband, Robert, was a wealthy carriage factory owner, and a generous, civic-minded one.

"I approached Luthera," Faith continued. "I asked her if she would be traveling back to Ottawa soon. She told me rather irately that she would of course stay to represent her father's company for the entire week."

"Who knows, maybe theirs was a marriage of convenience," Bertie said. "She might not be grieving for her husband at all."

"Does thee know where Luthera is staying?" I asked Faith.

"Yes. She's with the Clarkes. Georgia was there last night, too."

"Excellent. I might need to pay a visit on Georgia later today," I said. "I would like to know more about this Montgomery Carriage Company."

"I'll see what I can find out, as well." Bertie stood. "Now I must run, or the citizens of Amesbury will be waiting outside the post office ready to have my head."

"Thank thee for the buns, Bertie," I said and extended a hand. "And thank Sophie."

"I'll do that. Lovely to see you, Faith, darling." She squeezed my hand and made her way out.

"Did thee overhear anything else of use at the gathering?" I asked Faith.

"I'm not sure," my niece replied. "Ned Bailey was there seemingly trying to conduct some manner of business. He would corner this or that businessman and engage them in a hushed conversation, but I doubt he was successful. It's supposed to be a social affair. The daylight hours are for business, buying and selling and all that, the evenings for including the ladies and getting to know each other on a social level."

"How did William Parry act?"

"Officious, as usual." She raised a single eyebrow. "But I wondered if he was completely healthy. He kept coughing into his handkerchief."

"He might be ill. I saw him going into the tuberculosis doctor's office yesterday."

"Does it seem the disease is worsening of late, Rose? Spreading? I keep hearing of more and more people falling ill to it."

"I believe it is. Such ailments are often worse during the winter months, with all the houses shut up and wood and coal smoke being present. And for those weakened by the Asiatic influenza, consumption can be even more dangerous."

"That makes sense." Faith stood. "I'd better get myself off to work, too. Is thee feeling well, Rose?"

"Very well, indeed. And how is thy husband?"

"Also very well. Zeb has been busy with the Opening this week, though."

"That's right. He's moved up in the Parry company."

"I've barely seen him. He came home quite late last evening."

"What has he been busy with?" I asked. "Is he selling, or perhaps displaying the carriages in the showroom?"

"Some of both. Thee knows how well he speaks. He started out in manufacturing, but they quickly realized someone with his education and well-spoken manner would be better suited interacting with the public." She blushed. "Rose, I am blissfully happy, making a life with him."

"We are both truly blessed with our men, are we not?"

She hugged me. "Yes, we are."

As I tidied up the kitchen, I wished this case were tidier. I knew it wasn't my business. No one I was close to was being suspected. Still, if I could help Kevin in some way, I would like to. Right now, though, the facts were only dim figures in a thick fog.

TWELVE

ANNIE BEAUMONT LIFTED THE PINARD HORN from my bare belly an hour later. "The heartbeat is still fairly faint, but it's strong."

"Good." I'd asked my former apprentice and now my assistant to undertake my antenatal care. We sat in my office, which had its own outdoor entrance from the wide covered side porch of our home. David had designed it particularly to enable me to continue my business. It was decorated simply with a desk and swivel chair, a chaise, a sink for handwashing, and a small coal stove. I'd added rose-colored side curtains on the windows, with lace half curtains for my clients' privacy.

"It's a little early for a measurement, but we might as well," Annie continued. While I still reclined on the examination chaise with my skirts up, she stretched a measuring tape from my pubic bone to the top of my womb. She checked the measurement then glanced at my face as she told me the number. "This seems closer to five months than four, Rose. Are you sure of your dates?" She clapped her hand over her mouth, then laughed. "Look at me, asking the midwife if she's sure about the date of her last monthly."

"Annie, stop that." I smiled. "I'm in no position to be caring for my own pregnancy. Thee knows that is exactly the right question to ask a pregnant woman, whether it is me or someone else. In any event, it's possible my cycle was thrown off at the beginning with my body's new, ah, experiences." That is, enjoying glorious and frequent intimate acts with my husband. "If thee thinks the size of my uterus seems more appropriate for being five months gone, so be it." I pulled down my dress and sat up.

She made a note in my file. "You said you hadn't experienced early nausea. How are you feeling otherwise? Is your appetite healthy?"

"I am well. Better than well, truly. I'm eating heartily, and I feel extra energy, with my hair and fingernails strong and growing faster than usual." I shook my head. "I know our clients have reported the same, but it's quite remarkable to experience it in one's own self."

"Do you plan to stop riding your bicycle?" She tucked an errant red curl behind her ear.

"I will, as this creature grows." I gazed down at my belly and ran my hand over it.

"Then I think your pregnancy is proceeding in a healthy manner, Mrs. Dodge." The skin crinkled around her green eyes.

"And speaking of that. Annie, I would like to offer thee a partnership in my business."

Her eyebrows lifted nearly into her hairline. "Me?"

"Yes. Thee is fully capable of taking on clients of thine own, and I would like to work as equals with thee. We can work out the details, but does that interest thee?"

"Oh, Rose." She crossed her hands over her heart. "How far I have come. When I first met you, I couldn't even read."

She and Faith had worked at the Hamilton mill together, but both had had higher ambitions, other dreams to pursue.

"If Faith hadn't taught me my letters," she continued, "and if you hadn't taken me on as a student, this never would have happened." She sniffed and swiped at a tear.

"Well, it has. What does thee say?"

"I say yes. How else would I answer?" She reached out and gave me a quick hug, then sat again.

"It's about time for me to stop accepting new clients who will be due around the time my own child is due, or at least to let them know thee will be their primary midwife, not I."

Annie nodded.

"Thee can use my office here, and we can have new stationery and calling cards printed with both our names on them."

"My *memere* will never believe it." She frowned. "I should tell you, though, I have moved out of my family's rooms. I'm lodging at Mrs. Perkell's now."

"Oh? Why is that?" Virginia Perkell, Georgia Clarke's sister, kept a boardinghouse for young ladies. I myself had resided there until my sister died, then I'd joined my brother-in-law and the children at their home.

"Tuberculosis down in the Flats is running rampant. You know in what close quarters everyone lives."

The tenements at the Flats were mostly populated by immigrant families. French Canadians like Annie's, with her parents and siblings and her beloved *memere*, her mother's mother, all crammed into two rooms. Polish, Irish, and Italian families and workers lived in similar circumstances.

"I can't risk getting sick when I'm helping care for mothers-to-be and then their newborn infants," Annie added. "And Mrs. Perkell has a telephone should you need to summon me."

"It's a responsible move, and Virginia is an excellent housekeeper. I doubt thee will encounter illness there. Now, I think we should discuss our schedules."

"Which ladies are due the soonest?"

"Esther Ayensu on Carpenter Street ought to deliver within the next two weeks, three weeks at the most. It's her first, and I did the home visit yesterday. All seems to be in order."

We talked for a few minutes about another four women under our care.

Annie stood. "I'd better go. I have an errand to run for my mother."

"We'll speak soon."

She turned to go, then faced me again with a frown. "Rose, are you again helping the detective with this terrible murder?"

"I'm interested in it. As far as I know, not much information has yet come to light."

"My older brother Pierrot is a night watchman. He thinks he saw a man near where the body was found." She crossed herself. "May Mr. Harrington's soul rest in peace."

"The murderer, perhaps? That could be very useful information. I don't know where Justice's body was discovered."

"It was in the alley behind the opera house."

"Was it Pierrot who found the body?"

"Yes. He was quite disturbed by the experience. He didn't hear the shots, but when he was making his rounds an hour earlier there, he saw a tall fellow hurrying away."

"Has he told the police?"

"Not about the man. The thing is, Rose, Pierrot knows Faith's Zeb. And he thinks it might have been him he saw."

My mouth dropped open. *Zebulon Weed?* I shook my head, hard. "Zeb never would have murdered someone."

"I know that." She twisted her hands together. "You know that. But what if the police don't? We don't want to get him in trouble. And Faith would never forgive me."

I rose and took both her hands. "Thee must tell thy brother he has to go to Detective . . . I mean, Chief Donovan, and tell him what he saw. If it was Zeb, I'm sure he has a completely reasonable explanation. And there are plenty of other tall lanky men in town, especially this week."

"Maybe." She didn't sound convinced. "I suppose that is the right thing to do."

"Does thee want me to pass Kevin a word?"

"Would you? I'm not sure I can convince Pierrot to pay that visit on his own. My brother goes by Pete. Because people mangle the French, he took on an American nickname."

"Pete Beaumont. I've got it. Thank thee for telling me, Annie."

The door clicked shut behind her. I sank onto a chair, closed my eyes, and held Zeb in God's Light, praying a door hadn't clicked shut on his future.

THIRTEEN

I TELEPHONED THE POLICE STATION and left a message for Kevin that he might want to speak further with night watchman Pete Beaumont about what he saw the night of the murder. I explained where the family lived and left it at that. I had other calls to make, but those I wanted to do in person, and Orpha was on my list to visit, too.

I parked my bicycle in front of John Greenleaf Whittier's home on Friend Street as the town's bells chimed ten. It was a brisk morning, but I was warmed by my ride, and at least the bright skies didn't portend snow. Two years ago, we'd had a blizzard in late March, and once I'd seen snow on peach blossoms and daffodils in April. Anything could happen with New England weather at this time of year.

Friend John wasn't quite as old as my midwifery mentor, but he was increasingly frail and had been spending most of his time with his cousins in Danvers. He'd been a calm, wise voice in my life ever since I moved to Amesbury. I'd heard he was in town and wanted to share my happy news with him. He would likely surprise me with some tidbit of information about the investigation, too.

Mrs. Cate, his housekeeper, pulled open the door. "Oh, Mrs. Dodge, I'm glad you've come. Mr. Whittier is ailing something fierce. Perhaps you can lift his spirits."

Ailing? "I'm glad I came. In what way is he not well?"

She glanced behind her, then back at me, lowering her voice. "I think it's the melancholy more than anything. Claims he can't find the words anymore. You can go on into the study. He always enjoys your visits."

John sat in his rocking chair near the coal stove. He had a wool stocking cap atop his head, a blue wool shawl wrapped around his neck and shoulders, and a thick red plaid throw over his lap and legs, despite the warmth of the room.

"Rose, dear. Thee is a lovely sight for old, tired eyes. Do come in and sit with me." He folded the issue of the *Boston Globe* he'd been reading and laid it down.

"Hello, John. I am happy, as always, to see thee." I gently squeezed his bony hand before I sat, surprised at how cold his thin skin felt. "But thee looks chilled."

"It is true. I am never able to quite achieve a comfortable temperature in the colder months. But that's neither here nor there." He batted away his personal concerns. "What news does thee bring me from the outside world?"

Mrs. Cate popped her head in. "Can I get you both some hot tea?"

"Thank thee, Mrs. Cate," John said. "Rose?"

"I would love some." After the housekeeper left, I continued, "I have a bit of personal good tidings to share. With God's grace, David and I will be holding our first baby in about four months' time." I smiled.

"Why, that is splendid news, indeed." He bestowed a rare wide smile, stroking his snowy white chinstrap beard. "I am glad to hear it, and I have every confidence thee will make an excellent mother and thy husband a fine father. I am quite fond of children, as thee knows, despite never having sired any of my own."

"I do know." I remembered how he'd often winked at my young niece Betsy, even when we'd entered Meeting for Worship, even after John was already apparently in prayer on the facing bench reserved for elders.

"Why, just this week I penned a little poem for a woman who, as a girl, had always longed for my autograph but her father would not allow her to ask me," John said. "She's now a married woman and a neighbor of the Cartlands, with whom I reside in Danvers. Would thee like to hear the ending?"

"I would."

He gazed at the ceiling and recited,

> *I trace a name, then little known,*
> *Which since on many winds has blown,*
> *Glad to make good, however late,*
> *Her loss at such an early date,*
> *For which even now I almost pity her,*
> *By the best wish of,*
> *John G. Whittier*

"It's not much, but apparently my little ditty has made her very happy."

"It's a thoughtful gesture, John," I said.

"Such a short, silly piece is about all I can muster these days." He tented his fingers. "Now, I expect thee has come to seek counsel about the dastardly turn of events this week."

"I confess that is one of my purposes. Very little is known to date on who might have killed Justice Harrington, and why."

"Is that not the height of irony, that a man named Justice should have the ultimate unjust act committed upon him?" He raised his eyebrows.

"Yes. But it happened, nonetheless."

"Thy able detective has enlisted thy keen mind and insights, am I correct?"

"After a fashion," I said. "He's now the acting chief of police."

"Ah. I had not heard. He's up to the job, I'd say."

I only nodded. I'd been mistaken thinking John would have any useful information. He'd barely been in town.

"Shall we hold this situation in God's Light?" he asked.

I answered by folding my hands and closing my eyes. Praying with John never failed to be a deepening experience, no matter how long it lasted. I included Zeb in my circle of Light, that he be free from the taint of suspicion.

After only a couple of minutes, John cleared his throat. I opened my eyes to see him regarding me.

"Ned Bailey came to see me."

"About his motorcar scheme?" I asked.

"Yes. I'm an old man, Rose, and I can barely conceive of a motor-powered vehicle. Still, I've seen many inventions come to pass during my fourscore years. Why not a carriage that runs by its own power?"

Mrs. Cate set down a tray holding two full cups and saucers. "Well, I never." She straightened and folded her arms. "What? Will carriages be driving themselves around like some alien beings come down from the stars? I can't imagine what could possibly go wrong with that. Mark my words, Mr. Whittier." She raised an index finger in the air. "Only bad will come of this idea. And worse." She huffed her way out.

John's eyes twinkled as he sipped his tea. He murmured, "And there thee has the voice—and thoughts—of the common man and woman."

"I expect so. Motorcars would be quite a shift for society as a whole.

But in all seriousness, Ned also spoke to me of that plan only yesterday. Was he seeking thy counsel on the matter?"

"In truth, I'm not altogether sure of his purpose. I am a kind of town elder, I suppose, and he might have wanted my blessing. I advised him to go forth and create the future. I certainly won't be around to see it."

His words stabbed my heart. But, like Orpha, he was of advanced years, and no one lives forever. Still, I knew I would miss John keenly after his soul was released to God. I wrenched my thoughts from death back to motorcars. "Kevin says some sort of design plans went missing from Ned's uncle's home. I feel this has to be connected with the murder."

"Thee thinks this Justice might have made off with them and been murdered for his efforts?"

"Perhaps," I said slowly. "But why wouldn't Ned have had the plans in his own possession? Unless maybe they were the elder Bailey's plans that Ned himself absconded with."

"In which case Ned should have been the victim, not the Canadian."

"True."

"'Tis a pity this branch of Baileys does not share our faith, unlike thy brother-in-law, Frederick, and his family," John remarked. "They might more easily find their way to a peaceful settlement of their concerns."

"Yes." I agreed, but such wishful thinking wouldn't make it happen. "I also wondered if somehow William Parry is involved. The carriages from his factory have always been of a lesser quality. Perhaps he learned of some innovation and found a way to come into possession of its design."

"I daresay thee will solve this conundrum before the week is out." John drained his tea. "I'm afraid all this excitement has tired me, Rose. I'll have to free thee to continue on thy investigations."

I stood and took his extended hand, now only slightly warmer from the tea, in both of mine. "I shall see thee again soon. Be well, Friend."

"God willing, we will meet again."

FOURTEEN

"ROSE, DEAR," Georgia exclaimed after a maid showed me into the parlor of the fine home on Powow Street. "I'm pleased to see you."

"Good morning, Georgia," I said. "I hope thee is well."

"I am. Please sit." It was a tastefully appointed room, with plush rugs, rich window decor, and elegant furniture reflecting the family's comfortable financial position. The enticing smell of bread baking wafted in from the back of the house. "Do you know Mrs. Harrington?" Georgia asked.

Luthera, clad in what must be the stylish black dress Alma had described, sat on an embroidered settee. She bobbed her head at me. I perched on the brocade cushion of an upright chair.

"Yes, Ned Bailey introduced us only two days ago." I smiled at the Canadian. "Hello, Luthera."

She blinked at my use of her first name.

"So you've met Rose, that is, Mrs. Dodge." Georgia beamed.

"May I offer my condolences on the sudden loss of thy husband?" I asked Luthera.

"Thank you." She sniffed and held a black-trimmed handkerchief to her nose, but her eyes were not the red-rimmed ones of a new widow. She was also well-coiffed and her face nicely powdered.

"I expect Rose is already hard on the heels of the scoundrel who took Mr. Harrington's life." Georgia's eyes gleamed. "She's quite the private investigator."

Luthera gaped. I groaned inwardly as I held up my hand in a *stop* gesture. Georgia had several times previously become far too excited about the news of a murder, wanting me to share my detecting progress with her.

"In actuality, Luthera, I am a midwife, not a detective."

"But you work closely with the police, Rose," Georgia protested. "I know you do."

"I have several times in the past, it's true. But only as someone with whom the detective can discuss his ideas."

Georgia winked at me, as if we shared a secret.

47

"Isn't working with the police dangerous for a lady?" Luthera asked, her pale blue eyes wide. "Do murderers come after you because of what you know?"

"I do my best to stay out of harm's way." In fact, I had encountered danger in the past, and my life had been threatened more than once.

"Ladies should be able to do anything men do," Georgia went on. "Rose and I have worked toward suffrage for women. How is it where you live, Mrs. Harrington? Can ladies vote in Ottawa?"

"Women who own property may vote in municipal elections, and I have exercised my franchise to protect my family's business, in which I take an active part." Luthera sniffed with disdain. "But I am not a rabble-rouser and give little thought to the subject of suffrage."

Georgia raised her eyebrows and opened her mouth.

I thought it was time to change the topic of conversation. "Does thee have children?" I asked Luthera before Georgia could go on about our efforts to secure the vote.

"Mr. Harrington and I were married only last year and had not yet been blessed with offspring. Now I expect I never shall be." She let out a tragic sigh.

"There, there, Mrs. Harrington," Georgia said. "You are young and beautiful. After a suitable period of mourning, I know some dashing gentleman will offer you his hand, and you'll raise a passel of young ones."

Luthera raised her arm and held the back of her hand against her brow. "I am sure that will not come to pass, Mrs. Clarke."

I studied her. She feigned sorrow at the thought, but I doubted it was real.

"Georgia, how is thy passel?" I asked.

She laughed and smoothed back her white-streaked brown hair, done up today in a classic but somewhat out-of-fashion chignon. "They are blessedly all well, including little Rosie. Mrs. Dodge saved my life after I gave birth to my youngest," she told Luthera. "And we named the baby after her."

The long case clock in the entryway chimed eleven times.

Luthera stood and lifted her chin. "If you'll excuse me, I need to be getting into town for a meeting with prospective customers. My father's business continues regardless of personal tragedy."

I rose, too. "Shall I walk with thee?"

The corners of her mouth turned down. "Thank you, Mrs. Dodge, but I'm sure Mrs. Clarke will be supplying me with more suitable transportation."

"Yes, with pleasure." Georgia rang a little bell. When the maid arrived, Georgia said, "Please have Wilson bring the buggy around for Mrs. Harrington."

"Thank you," Luthera said. "I'll fetch my hat and my reticule. It was pleasant to visit with you, Mrs. Dodge."

I doubted she had actually found it so. "I was glad for the chance, Luthera. I hope the rest of thy stay is uneventful. When will thee be traveling back north?"

"It is not yet certain. Good day."

I sat again after she disappeared into the hall, the clicking of her heels on the stairs growing fainter as she ascended.

"Well, well, Rose." Georgia clasped her hands in her lap. "Now you can tell me what you know."

"I am more interested in what thee knows." I leaned closer and murmured, "About thy guest."

"Let's wait a moment, shall we?" She cast her gaze upward, from whence came footsteps returning down the stairs.

Luthera, now clad in coat, gloves, and a different, fur-trimmed hat, with one hand in a fur muff, said from the doorway, "I shall return at the end of the day, Mrs. Clarke." She raised a gloved hand.

"Farewell, Mrs. Harrington." Georgia waited until the front door clicked shut after Luthera. "What do you mean, what I know about her?"

"For example, I heard she was at the soiree last evening. What about the night before? Did she stay out late? Was thee with her then?"

"Let's see, now." Georgia tapped her mouth, thinking. "Why, no, I wasn't. The Harringtons were at the banquet, of course. My oldest was feeling poorly, and I decided to stay at home to comfort him. He's nine but still appreciates his mama's affection. I hope he always will."

"Did thee notice what time Luthera returned?" I asked. Obviously Justice didn't return with her. He was lying dead in an alley.

"No. But I can ask Wilson when he returns what time he brought them home. Oh! I mean her."

"Wilson is thy driver?"

"Yes, and he does all manner of other tasks around here. He's an entirely competent and genteel man."

"I would appreciate thee inquiring of him. In a discreet manner, naturally."

"Rose." Georgia grasped my hand. "You can't think Mrs. Harrington would kill her own husband, can you?"

"One must suspect everyone at this stage in an investigation. Perhaps she stands to benefit from his death. They could have had an unhappy marriage, short as it was. Or he might have been abusing her in private. We don't know." And Luthera was a tall woman with a slender shape. In the dark, she might be mistaken for a tall lean man wearing a long coat. If the person Pierrot saw had been Zeb, I prayed he had a good explanation for his presence in the alley.

"But surely others would have had more cause than his wife to end Mr. Harrington's life," Georgia protested.

"That's also entirely possible."

She nodded, then gazed with a little smile at my waist. "Rose Dodge, I think you've been holding out on me. Are you carrying a child?"

I smiled back. "As it happens, I am. And this week everyone seems to be noticing. I guess I'm finally showing my condition, as the phrase goes."

"Indeed you are, and I couldn't be happier for you. You'll be giving birth in the summertime, I wager."

"Thee is correct." I rose. "I must be off, but I wonder if I might avail myself of thy water closet before I continue."

"Any time, my dear. I know well the urge to relieve oneself when one carries around an increasingly full womb. It's under the stairs."

"Please telephone me after thee speaks with thy manservant."

"I will. And you be careful out there."

"Have no fear." I supposed everyone telling me to be cautious went hand in hand with people noticing my gravid state. So be it. I had no intention of coming to bodily harm, or worse.

FIFTEEN

AFTER A REST AT HOME AND A BITE TO EAT, I ventured out again toward Carriage Hill. All the factories were hosting open-door showrooms this afternoon. If I paid a visit to the Parry and Bailey displays, I might be able to learn something. And I very much wanted to speak with Zeb in private, if I could.

I left my cycle at home and strolled instead of riding. I passed the bustling TW Lane carriage manufacturer on Elm Street and kept going up the hill to the Parry factory on Chestnut Street. The broad doors were flung all the way open, despite the brisk air, and people bustled about. Several vehicles stood outside for viewing. As a man regarding a surrey spit to the side, I covered my mouth and gave him a wide berth. I'd read that physicians in New York City had implored their public health department to ban public expectoration. The department had complied by widely circulating a leaflet cautioning against the germ-spreading practice. I wished Amesbury would follow suit, or perhaps the Commonwealth would enact a law to that effect.

I meandered inside. The latest innovations in carriage design were displayed, from a bright red governess wagon to a four-person closed Rockaway with the wheel cutout that allowed for easier turning. A section along the back wall held various structural components, half of which I didn't know the function of.

The crowd was made up mostly of men. The smell of tobacco and hair pomade scented the air, but it was diluted by the chill breeze coming in from outside. A few women perused the wares, and I glimpsed Luthera among them, deep in conversation with William Parry across the room. She certainly seemed to be devoted to her father's business.

I wandered among the vehicles. I supposed after our baby grew into a child, and definitely after more children came along, David and I would want to purchase a carriage larger than his two-person doctor's buggy. But surely not one manufactured by Parry and company. A Bailey or a Clarke carriage would be of higher quality.

I stroked the high wheel on a runabout, casting my gaze over the gathering. *Ah*. In the far corner stood Zeb, an arched undercarriage part in his hands, looking like he was explaining it to a portly gentleman. I headed in that direction, but I didn't get far before William Parry intercepted me.

"Mrs. Dodge, good afternoon. Shopping for a new carriage, are we?" He beamed. "This runabout is a fine vehicle for a lady to drive. Easy to handle, not too large."

"It's a very nice carriage, but I'm not looking to purchase at this moment, no." I gestured around the room. "This open house looks very well attended."

"Yes, indeed. I venture a guess that we are drawing more interest this week than is any other firm."

Unlikely, I thought, but I kept my opinion to myself. "That will be good for thy business. If thee will excuse me, I want to say hello to my friend Zebulon."

"Mr. Weed is a most excellent fellow to have about. Most excellent. He has quite the way with customers."

I made my way to Zeb and waited, gazing at the wall of component parts until the man with whom he was speaking turned away.

"Rose, what a nice surprise," Zeb said. "Thee is looking well."

"As is thee, Zeb, and making some sales, by the looks of it."

"I'm doing my best." He lowered his voice. "I'd rather be working for Robert Clarke or the Baileys. The quality of their products is much superior."

"I would have to agree with thee."

He frowned at me and continued to speak softly. "But thee isn't here to buy a carriage. Thee must have heard of Justice Harrington's death. Is thee investigating his murder?"

"I admit I'm attempting to gather a few facts to help the police."

"An avocation at which thee excels."

"Zeb," I matched his soft tone. "One thing I've learned is that a night watchman saw thee in the very alley where the body was found. On that same night. I know thee wasn't involved in the death, but can thee tell me what thee was doing there?"

"No," he said in a rush. The smile slid off his face and his expression turned grim. "I was doing nothing. I wasn't there. This watchman is lying."

I opened my mouth to object but closed it before I spoke. Despite sensing that it was Zeb who lied, it wasn't my place or business to challenge his account. Let Kevin do that.

I touched his arm. "I'm glad to hear thee was far from the violent deed." Had Annie's brother in fact lied? But why? And what was the reason for Zeb's grim look?

His nostrils flared as he caught sight of something over my shoulder.

Oh. Kevin suddenly stood at my elbow, in a gray serge suit instead of a uniform. I'd apparently conjured him up by merely thinking of him. But no uniform? Perhaps civilian attire was what a chief of police was supposed to wear. Or maybe he was trying not to be conspicuous as an officer of the peace. Which was all very well for the strangers to town, but anyone from Amesbury well knew Kevin's profession.

"I'm surprised to see you here, Miss Rose." Kevin clasped his hands behind his back. "Good afternoon, Mr. Weed."

"Greetings, Detective." Zeb bobbed his head. "If thee isn't here to purchase a carriage, I'll be off to my customers."

"Actually, Weed, I'd like to have a word with you," Kevin said, his voice steely. "In private, if we might."

Uh-oh.

Zeb's eyes shifted left and right, as if he wanted to escape. Had I sealed his fate by passing along Pete's report? It would kill Faith if Zeb were guilty of any misdeed. The ultimate violent act of homicide? I couldn't even imagine how she would react. Or . . . perhaps I could.

"Two Quakers and a detective, is it?" William Parry said from a few paces away.

His tone was hearty, but his visage countered it. The factory owner looked either nervous or worried. I couldn't tell which

"What can we help you with today, Mr. Donovan?" William went on. "I hear you're now heading up our fine department of boys in blue, as it were."

"Mr. Parry, I have a little matter to clear up with Weed here," Kevin replied. "Can you spare him for a few minutes?"

"Of course, of course," William said. "In fact, you can use my office. Mr. Weed knows where it is. Anything to help keep the peace in our fair town."

Zeb cast me a desperate glance before leading Kevin through a door to the side of the showroom.

"Has my best young salesman done something wrong, Mrs. Dodge?" The worried expression was gone. William sounded downright jovial. "Only a criminal act would merit the attentions of our chief of police."

"No." I gave him my sternest look. "Zeb is an honest and law-abiding person, William. I won't hear of thee even mentioning the idea of him committing a crime." Even though I was the one responsible for bringing Kevin here.

"Very well, then, Mrs. Dodge. I suppose you're putting your best detective skills to work solving this wretched killing that has threatened to derail our entire Spring Opening."

"Not at all." I kept my voice level. "I'm simply caring for ladies bringing new life into the world, as I do. Good day, William."

He nodded, but he'd narrowed his eyes, and his gaze was on the closed door to his office. The concerned look had returned. Why did I have the feeling he was worried for himself, not for his employee?

SIXTEEN

DAVID AND I DROVE IN THE BUGGY to my brother-in-law's home at six o'clock. It wasn't too far, but the night had turned colder, and we'd be returning home not until after the family dinner Frederick and his new wife, Winnie, had invited us to.

"I stopped in at Orpha's this afternoon, but Alma said she was in a deep sleep," I said. "David, I fear she might slip away any day now."

"That is the way of it." He shifted the reins to one hand and patted the thick driving blanket covering our legs. "You'll miss her deeply."

"I shall."

"Will Faith and Zeb be at the house tonight, do you think?" he asked.

"I don't know." I held on as we jostled over a bumpy section of Sparhawk Street. "So much happened today I wanted to discuss with thee."

"About the murder investigation?"

"Yes, mostly." I twisted my gloved hands together. "One part of it is that Annie's brother Pete, a night watchman, apparently saw Zeb that night in the same alley where the body was found. This afternoon I popped into the Parry showroom to speak with Zeb, but Kevin showed up and took him off for a chat in private."

"Zeb? He's a fine, upstanding young man, and a Quaker, to boot. He wouldn't have killed anyone."

"Never. But when I asked him about what Pete related, he said the man was lying, that he hadn't been there. He got a rather grim look on his face when he said it. I'm worried about what he might be hiding."

"Don't you think Faith probably knows?" He clucked to Daisy to turn onto Center Street.

"I'm not sure. She told me he's been working late this week during the Spring Opening."

"Kevin Donovan is a good man. He won't haul Zeb in on false charges."

"I hope not." Kevin had made mistakes before. He'd better not this time. We pulled up in front of the Baileys' modest house, which I had called home for several years. My oldest nephew, Luke, trotted down the front steps. At fifteen, he was still growing and was as much of a beanpole as always. His voice had stopped cracking, though, and was now a pleasant baritone.

"I'll see to Daisy, David. Here, Aunt Rose. Let me help you down." Luke extended his hand.

"Thank thee, dear Luke." I kissed his cheek once I reached the ground, then left the two of them to unhitch the sleek roan mare and put her in with Star, Frederick's horse. I made my way through the side door into a warm kitchen fragrant with roasting meat. I also spied apple pies cooling on a shelf.

"Winnie," I said to the plump aproned woman at the stove. "These pies are works of art and they smell heavenly." One had strips of crust woven into a lattice, and the other was decorated with stars cut out of pastry dough.

She turned and smiled. "Hello, Rose, darling. Those beauties are Mark's doing."

Nephew Mark, now twelve, had become interested in cooking last year. His twin, Matthew, didn't share the drive to create delicious food.

"How is thee?" Winnie asked.

"I am well, thank thee. This wee one is growing apace." I patted my full waist.

"As it well might. I'm glad to hear it."

"Will Faith and Zeb be here?"

"No." She leaned down and drew a large pan of scalloped potatoes out of the oven, nicely browned on top, and set it at the edge of the stove. "She said they're both busy with the Opening. Terrible news about that poor Canadian, isn't it?"

"Yes."

Winnie wiped her hands on her apron. "Rose, I heard a disturbing rumor at the market this afternoon." She glanced toward the door to the sitting room and lowered her voice to a whisper. "I overheard someone saying the police think Zeb might be the killer. That has to be wrong. How could they think he might have committed such an evil act?"

"A night watchman spied him in the alley, that's how." I let out a breath. "My detective friend, now the acting chief, talked to Zeb this afternoon, but I don't know what came of the conversation. I agree, Zeb wouldn't hurt a soul." I removed my cloak and hat and hung them, then sank onto a chair at the already-set table.

David and Luke hurried in from outside, and Winnie and David exchanged greetings. David pulled off his gloves and shed his coat, while Luke went to the pump in the sink to wash his hands.

"It looks like you've outdone yourself, Winnie," David said with a smile.

Betsy, now ten, rushed in from the front. "Auntie Rose, Uncle David!" She wrapped David in the biggest hug, blond curls escaping her long braid.

"Hello, sweet Betsy," I said to her, but I made my way to Luke at the back of the kitchen.

"Thee knows Annie's older brother, doesn't thee?" I asked him in a low voice.

"Pete? Sure." He wiped his hands on a towel. "He was helping with our ragtag baseball team last summer. He's a night watchman now."

"I know. Would thee say he is an honest type?"

"I think so." My nephew cocked his head. "Why does thee ask?"

"It's complicated." If Pete had told an untruth, why? And if he hadn't, that meant Zeb was lying, with an even bigger *why* hanging unanswered.

"Is this about the murder?" His eyes widened.

"Frederick, boys," Winnie called to the other room. "Rose and David are here, and dinner is ready."

"It might be," I murmured.

SEVENTEEN

IN THE BUGGY IN FRONT OF ALMA'S HOUSE, I turned toward David at a few minutes before eight. We'd finished our pie with the Baileys when the telephone had rung in the other room. Frederick answered and summoned me, saying it was Alma. My heart went heavy as I rose and went to the device in the sitting room. I had told Alma this afternoon where I would be during the evening.

"I think you'd better come now, Rose," she'd said in a low, somber tone.

I'd returned to the table and told the family. We all held Orpha in a moment of silent prayer before David drove me over to Orchard Street.

Now I kissed my husband. "I might be all night," I said. "Don't wait up for me."

"I shall sleep near the telephone. Summon me whenever you're ready to come home. I will hold Orpha in my prayers even as I slumber."

I gazed fondly at him before stepping down and entering the house. Alma sat darning a stocking at Orpha's bedside when I crept in. She raised a tearstained face.

"I knew this time was coming. But it's hard, Rose." She sniffed and dabbed at her eyes with a handkerchief.

I touched her shoulder. "I know." I'd accompanied my sister Harriet on her last journey. She'd been much younger than Orpha and had been felled by illness, not old age. Still, it was those who were left behind who felt the hurt of loss.

I gazed at my teacher and friend in the bed, this woman who had been an important part of my adult life in myriad ways. She lay on her back with her eyes shut. I stood with my own eyes closed for a moment, holding her soul in God's Light that her passage might be easy.

"Alma, let me relieve thee. Has thee supped?"

"No."

"Then go. Eat and go to bed. I'll be here for the duration."

"I'll eat something." Alma stood. "I doubt I could sleep, though. I did clean her up an hour ago. She's not passing much water, but I fitted her out with extra rags."

"Has she been in pain, that thee can tell?"

58

"I don't think so. She's not grimacing nor groaning, but she doesn't seem conscious. It's different than being asleep."

"Yes, she's in a comatose state, Alma."

She kissed Orpha's brow and whispered, "I love you, Nana," before making her way quietly out of the room.

I smoothed Orpha's hair back off her forehead before I sat, then took her hand in mine. My mentor's life ending. My baby's life beginning. So much change in the world—for good, for bad, for whatever we humans would make of it.

"Thy passage will be easy, dear Orpha," I murmured. "Thee will glide away on a soft wave and leave this earthly shell behind. I love thee, and it's all right to let go." I kept talking until I ran out of soothing words. I didn't know if she could hear me or, if she could, if she could make sense of my ramblings. But I had the notion my voice might bring her comfort. I began to sing and started with, "Lullaby, and good night, with roses bedight."

Alma came back in after some time and pulled the rocker on the other side of the bed closer to it. She took Orpha's other hand and joined me in a soft rendition of "Shenandoah," harmonizing in a sweet soprano that fit well with my lower alto range.

"Has thee had voice lessons?" I asked her after we'd finished another tune.

She laughed quietly. "I did, for a time, before I married. Prudence Weed taught me. Once the babies came along, it seemed more practical to take up dressmaking than to pursue a career as a singer."

I tilted my head. "Does Prudence have a son named Zeb?"

"Yes. Faith's Zeb."

"I forgot you know Faith. I guess I didn't realize Zeb's mother taught music." I checked Orpha, but our chatting didn't seem to have disturbed her.

"Mrs. Weed doesn't teach anymore." Alma raised her eyebrows and turned her mouth down a little. "She's overly fond of the drink, that one. She would be late for lessons, and one morning she was clearly inebriated. My father threw her out of the house."

Good heavens. I brought a hand to my mouth. "I had no idea."

"It's a pity. She has a beautiful voice and has performed onstage. Mrs. Weed was also a good teacher—when she wasn't more soused than a sailor."

59

Prudence was a Quaker as far as I knew, and we were cautioned not to imbibe. If she hadn't been raised in the Religious Society of Friends, it was unlikely Zeb's father would have married her. The strictures on Quakers marrying out were easing of late but they wouldn't have been twenty-five or thirty years ago. Even I had been read out of Meeting after marrying Unitarian David, but I had appealed and been readmitted within two months' time. What was Prudence doing becoming intoxicated — or drinking alcohol at all? Faith must know. She and Zeb had lived with his parents for a few months after they'd married. I would ask her next time we met.

Alma and I lapsed into silence. After a bit I glanced over to see her sleeping in the chair. Good. It might be a long night. In my midwifery practice, I was accustomed to sitting up all night with a woman bringing new life into the world. Helping her through her labor, assisting her to walk the floors, supporting her squats to help bring down the baby, or even simply sitting by her side as she snoozed between pains. I could easily manage an end-of-life sitting up, too. The full moon shone in above the half curtain, lighting Orpha's way into the next world.

I slipped out for a moment to use the water closet. When I returned, my teacher's breathing had become noisy. Her mouth hung open, and her eyes had cracked open, as well. She took in a breath, and when the next didn't come, I wondered if it had been her last. Should I call Mary Chatigny? She'd asked to be notified. But I didn't know what she could do. It was growing late, and despite Mary's vow to her mother, I felt accompanying Orpha was my job, and Alma's.

With a gasping inhale, Orpha finally took another breath. This continued for an hour. I tracked the seconds between breaths, exactly as I sometimes counted the seconds between a birthing woman's contractions. Alma stayed sleeping. I did not wake her.

Finally, my teacher had no more breaths to take. As I watched, the pink slid out of her skin. I knew her soul had been released from her earthly shell, too, but that was less visible. The clock on the bureau ticked from eleven fifty-nine to twelve as if nothing had happened. I ran my hand over Orpha's hair one last time, slid her eyelids shut, and kissed her forehead. I straightened the covers, smoothing them over her chest.

"And thus it is, dear Orpha," I murmured, removing my spectacles and setting them on the bedside table. I sat, holding her in God's Light. When quiet tears flowed from my closed lids, I did not wipe them away.

I didn't know how long it had been when I felt something stirring within me, as if some small fish had flipped and rippled along the walls of its tank. Except this was my baby. I hadn't yet felt it move. Clients of mine had described the sensation, and now I truly knew what they meant. I hoped the quickening was a sign that part of Orpha's spirit had jumped into the tiny life within me. I couldn't imagine any better parting gift.

EIGHTEEN

"HER SOUL LEFT HER BODY at a few minutes before midnight, David," I told him after he helped me up into the buggy at an hour past dawn the next morning. "Alma slept through the death, but I finally woke her. We washed Orpha and prepared her. By the time we were done, it was nearly two o'clock and I decided to sleep there for a bit, borrowing the girls' bed."

"You are a most caring friend, my darling."

I blinked away more tears. "I was honored to accompany her to her death."

We rode in silence until we reached our house.

"I'm going straight on to the hospital if you don't mind," he said, "but I'll come home early today to comfort you."

"That's fine, and I will welcome thee." I touched his hand. "I have a bit of happy news to share with thee first. Last night as I sat after she died, I felt our baby move." I smiled through my fatigue and grief. "It was the first time."

He threw his arms around me and murmured into my hair, "That makes me very happy."

"Me, as well." I sat comforted by the warmth of his arms for a moment, then disengaged. "It means the little one continues healthy. By and by, as it grows, thee will be able to feel it kick, but not yet."

David sat beaming at me. Daisy nickered. The milkman's white wagon pulled up. The day's young sun slanted across the road and through the bare branches of a tall elm.

"Go on and get thyself to work. I'm going to try to grab a little more sleep before my morning clients come." I kissed him and climbed down.

Inside, I put away the milk. I washed my face and hands, used the lavatory, and let down my hair. Ravenous, I scrambled two eggs. I toasted bread and fried a slice of ham to go with the eggs. I sipped a cup of herbal tea instead of coffee but found myself buzzing with thoughts and feelings instead of relaxing into rest.

The feelings were easy to identify. Grief dragged me down. My body was heavy with it. How I would miss Orpha's twinkling eyes, her raucous laugh, her wise counsel about all things connected to pregnancy and birth, life and death. Perhaps most of all I was going to miss when she peered into my soul. She had a way of seeing the true me—sometimes before I myself was even aware of what I was experiencing.

But my mentor's days had run their course. At least her spirit hadn't been cut short by illness or violence. It was in the right order of things that old people should die. We humans had no way of stopping that natural progression, nor should we.

Justice Harrington's life, however, had not been allowed to follow its own path. I wasn't surprised my thoughts led me, even as I grieved, to seek his killer. I brought my tea into the office as my grandmother's clock struck eight. I wanted to gather my thoughts, and I'd found in the past that laying them out in writing could prove useful.

First, though, I needed to telephone Mary Chatigny. I put the call through to Gertrude, the operator, and waited until Mary answered.

"Mary, I need to tell thee that Orpha's soul was released to God last night. Alma and I were with her. She died only minutes before midnight."

I was met with silence. I hoped she wasn't upset with me for not summoning her.

"May her blessed soul rest in peace," Mary finally said. "She went quietly?"

Perhaps the good doctor had been praying instead of speaking. "Yes. When I arrived, she was already in a comatose state, and she didn't seem to be in pain or struggling. After she was gone, Alma and I washed her and laid her out. I'm not sure what the arrangements are now. We were both so exhausted we simply went to sleep at around two in the morning."

"I'll handle that. Mrs. Latting and I have an undertaker arranged. Don't worry. Thank you for being her death midwife, odd as that sounds." She gave a low laugh.

"It does, doesn't it? I might have to add it to the letterhead on my business stationery."

We were both quiet for another moment. I thought about her own letterhead. "Mary, I think thee has a patient named Marie Deorocki. She's a friend of mine and seems ill with coughing. I heard a rale when she breathed. I'm concerned that she's still going about town, making purchases and conducting business."

"I shouldn't talk to you about patients, but you are correct. Mrs. Deorocki is ill with tuberculosis. I'm concerned, too. For her own health, and she also could be infecting others. But she refuses to stay home and rest. And she won't hear of traveling to a sanitarium."

"That's a pity."

"If you can persuade her otherwise, it would be a great service to her and her fellow citizens."

"I'll try." I watched a scarlet cardinal hop on the railing of my porch. "Does William Parry have the disease, too?"

"Mrs. Dodge, I truly can't reveal anything else about my patients. It's all to be confidential."

"I understand. Please let me know if thee needs my help with Orpha or anything else."

"I shall do so. I expect she's now in heaven having a good laugh and a piece of berry pie with my mother. That's a comforting thought, isn't it?"

"It is."

We said our farewells and ended the call. I didn't have as clear an image of the afterlife as that held by practitioners of other religions or even some of my fellow Friends. I did have faith that Orpha's soul was resting easy, wherever it had landed. I resolved to make my own mind easy about the unsettling events of this week. Only then would I be able to rest.

After I laid out a fresh sheet of paper and sharpened a pencil, I began to jot down what I knew, as well as which questions remained.

Justice shot. Where is the gun? Who killed him? Did wife abuse him?
Luthera. Reason to want husband dead?
The stolen plans. Ned's? Plans for what, exactly?
Night watchman saw tall person running. Zeb? Who? Need to talk to Pete. If Zeb, why?
William Parry. Heard arguing with Justice. Is William involved? Why?

I sat back. What else did I know, or need to know? I thought of one more item.

Wilson, Georgia's driver. What time did he bring Luthera home?

The bell in the hall sounded, the one attached to the twisting handle in the front door.

"Rose?" Faith called from outside. She pounded at the entrance.

"Just a minute," I called as I hurried to pull open the door. "Faith, come in."

"I can't. But . . ." Her voice trailed off. Her bonnet was askew, and her cheeks were flushed.

"What's wrong?"

"It's Zeb. They think he—" Her words rushed out, ending in a sob. She brought a shaking hand to her mouth.

"Step inside, dear Faith. It's cold, and thee is upset." I pulled her in, shutting the door. I kept hold of her arm and persuaded her to perch on the settee in the sitting room next to me. "Now, take a deep breath and tell me what has happened."

"I tried to call thee last night, but no one answered. Kevin Donovan questioned Zeb yesterday. Someone claimed he saw Zeb the night of the murder."

"I know," I said in a soft voice.

"Thee does?" She stared at me.

"I was at the Parry showroom yesterday afternoon when Kevin arrived, saying he needed to speak with Zeb in private."

"But Rose! Zeb is a gentle man. He never would hurt anyone, ever."

"Faith, calm thyself." I took her hand. "Did Kevin arrest him?"

"No."

"Did he detain him at the police station?"

She shook her head.

"That means Zeb is not in trouble." *Yet.* "That said, does thee feel he hides anything from thee? Does thee know if he was out late working that night, or was he perhaps doing something different about which he didn't want to inform thee?"

Faith let out a noisy breath and reclaimed her hand, clasping it with the other in her lap. "I've never told thee, but his mother has a terrible habit of drinking alcohol, and far too much of it."

"Prudence." Exactly what Alma had said.

"Yes. I know about her habit, because we lived with them for a time. But Zeb is desperately unhappy about it. He's worried about her, and he feels ashamed, too. I think he might have been out helping her the night of the murder."

"Has thee asked him directly?"

"No." She glanced at the clock, which read eight forty-five. "Criminy."

"Faith . . ." I gently scolded her for using a euphemism for Christ.

"I know. I shouldn't utter that word. But I have to be at the newspaper office at nine." She stood. "Thank thee for listening, Rose. I pray thee is working hard on the case."

"As hard as I can. As is Kevin, I can assure thee."

Faith tossed her head as if she didn't believe me. "He needs to be looking in an entirely different direction, in my opinion."

NINETEEN

AFTER FAITH LEFT, I returned to my office. I hadn't even had the chance to tell her about Orpha. That news could wait. I'd resumed staring at my list when Akwasi Ayensu rapped on my office door.

Esther's tall, dark husband worried his cap in his large hands. "Rose, Esther believes the baby is coming. She needs you." Despite Akwasi attending Amesbury Friends' worship, John Whittier hadn't been successful in convincing him to adopt our rather archaic ways of speaking.

I wasn't surprised at his words. The full moon often brought on labor. "I'll come straight away," I said. "Go and sit with her. Smooth her brow, hold her hand. Persuade her to take deep slow breaths during the pains. Can thee do that?"

"I will do anything for her." His expression of worry made his ears stick out from his head even more than usual. "But isn't it too early for the baby?"

"Not too. Esther is within what we call the safe period of time for birth. Thy baby is well big enough to survive outside the womb."

"He is?" His deep brown eyes widened, and he allowed himself a little smile.

"Yes. Off with thee now. I'll be along within the half hour."

He clapped his cap onto his head and rushed away. I didn't hurry as I changed my dress, pinned up my hair again, checked my birthing satchel. This was a first birth and was unlikely to speed along. When a woman's body hadn't yet stretched all the way open to let out a baby even once, labor was usually somewhat prolonged. I was glad I'd had a big breakfast. It occurred to me that I'd never asked if Esther was willing to speak with Kevin about the argument she'd overheard. It was too late, now.

I put in a call to Annie at Mrs. Perkell's. "Esther Ayensu is in labor. Can thee meet me at the house?" I gave her the number on Carpenter Street.

"Yes. I'll be there shortly."

"I doubt it's urgent. Take time to eat something. It's her first, and we could be there for many hours." I rang off and lettered a notice for my morning's clients, saying I had been summoned to a birth, and we would reschedule their appointments. After I fixed it to the outside of my office door, I scribbled a note to David about my whereabouts, donned my shoes and cloak, and set off to do what I did best. I'd have to leave solving the murder to Kevin, and rightly so. And postpone my rest, as well.

I was halfway there, feeling lightheaded from my fatigue, when I realized my hands were also light. I'd forgotten my satchel. I shook my head in disbelief. I was on my way to a birth, after all. Reversing direction, I walked back down nearly the entire length of Whittier Street. A chickadee buzzed from an oak tree under the slate-colored sky. I sniffed the air, picking up the metallic scent of impending snow.

As I passed Bertie's cottage, which was tucked behind a larger mansard-roofed home, she emerged from the back leading her horse, Grover.

"What ho, Rose?" She smiled at me. "Out for your morning constitutional?"

"Not exactly. I was on my way to a birth on Carpenter Street, but I forgot my birthing satchel."

"Is this Rose Carroll Dodge or some alien being inhabiting your body?" She peered into my face. "You never forget your bag of tricks. Is your condition addling your brilliant brain?"

"That's possible. But it's more that . . ." My voice trailed off as my throat thickened with emotion. I swallowed it down. "Oh, Bertie. Orpha died last night."

Bertie quickly tied the horse to a hitching post and held out her arms. "Poor Rosetta."

I let her hug me. Her embrace felt nearly as good as David's had. I sniffed and pulled apart. "She was old. It was her time."

"I know. But she was a wise old woman, and we need those in our lives. And you loved her. I'm sorry, my dear." She pulled a clean folded handkerchief out of her skirt pocket and handed it to me.

"Thank thee." I dabbed my eyes.

"Say, did I tell you I reconciled with my own not-so-wise old woman?"

"Thy mother?" I knew Bertie had been estranged from her mother for some years.

She nodded. "I decided to let past hurts stay in the past where they belong. I'm quite enjoying getting to know the old bag again."

"Thy mother must be a pip. Look who she raised." I swiped away the rest of my tears.

"She is." A black gelding clopped by pulling a late-model phaeton. Grover whinnied at the horse. "Sure are a lot of carriages around this week. The Board of Trade even hauled Sophie in to translate for a couple of the visitors."

"Because of her Portuguese?"

"Yes. She grew up speaking it with her daddy. And now she's interpreting for a handsome green-eyed Brazilian gent and a man from Lisbon. Although the Brazilian speaks English well enough, as she discovered."

"I think I might have seen the Brazilian around."

"He's quite the charmer."

With a start, I remembered my mission, as well as the time. "Bertie, why isn't thee at the post office?"

"I was just headed down there. My assistant opens up on Thursdays. There's no rush."

I thought. Bertie had her finger on the pulse of the town. "Has thee heard anything of interest about the murder?"

"You haven't solved it yet?" She elbowed me with a grin.

"Goodness, no."

"As a matter of fact, I might have a tidbit for you," she said. "I heard the Parry factory might be closing down. They're in some kind of financial straits."

"Interesting. What kind of straits?"

"Don't know." Bertie cocked her head. "Maybe despair pushed Mr. Parry to kill the Canadian."

"But why?"

"Ah, that's for you and your detective to ferret out."

"I was at the Parry open house yesterday," I said. "All seemed well with the business. If they close, Faith's Zeb would be out of a job, more's the pity."

"Zeb Weed. Prudence's son." Bertie frowned. "I read the name in the newspaper just now."

My eyes widened. "Zeb's or Prudence's?"

"No, not the Quaker sot."

I nearly reeled from the description. "Thee knows she drinks?"

"Everybody does. Once upon a time I would enjoy a spot of sherry with her. But her spot always turned into the whole bottle. She can get unpleasant under those circumstances."

"I wonder how I only learned of her predilection this week." It was truly curious I'd never heard even a whisper about Prudence's overindulgence in drink.

"Because you're a good Quaker, Rose, who refrains from imbibing, and you have other things to do with your life than gossip. At any rate, it was her son whose name I read in the *Amesbury Chronicle*," Bertie went on. "The article said Zebulon Weed is a person of interest in the homicide."

"But Faith said he hasn't been detained by the police or charged with anything. Thee knows they must be wrong about him."

"I don't know the fellow, Rose. Everyone has their dark side. I hope for your family's sake he's innocent, though. Now, I thought you had a birth to get to."

TWENTY

ESTHER'S LABOR WAS GOING ALONG MUCH FASTER than labors progressed for many first-time mothers. Annie and I exiled Akwasi out back to his carpentry shop after he hovered in the bedroom, looking worried and helpless. Esther said she wanted to walk. Annie and I took turns walking circuits through the small home, stopping with her to concentrate on a contraction when it came. She was quiet and stoic about the pain, focusing inward on her body.

I pushed any thoughts of Zeb having a dark side into the back of my brain. I was here to be a midwife, not a detective. And every time I felt grief for Orpha rise up, I pushed it back down, as well. She would be the first to tell me that, during a labor, the mother-to-be was more important than our personal lives.

As we paused in the kitchen for a pain, Esther's gaze fell on the calligraphy cards and supplies on the table. After the contraction passed, she spoke.

"Rose, if I don't survive, will you make sure the Board of Trade pays Akwasi for my work?"

"Nonsense. Thee will survive." It was true, some women did not make it through a birth alive, but Esther would not be one of them. She was healthy and young enough, and I had a good feeling about this labor.

"I thought I had time to finish up the week," she went on. "Mr. Parry asked for a special set of cards last week, which I completed. He hasn't paid me, either. Please promise me."

"Very well." Anything to set her mind at ease.

"I think Parry is kind of a . . . oh." She groaned low as another contraction began. She bent over and leaned her forearms on the table. When the pain was finished, she straightened and picked up where she'd left off. "He's a weasel. Possibly a scoundrel. Don't tell anyone I said so, though."

I laughed. "I promise that, too." I didn't have time to think about Parry right now, but I filed away her opinion for later. We resumed our walking until the pains were coming fast and furious. "Let's get thee back to the bedroom. I think this baby is coming." Her bag of waters had not yet broken, but that wasn't a problem. In fact, the cushion of the water would provide for a more gentle birthing.

Annie and I helped her through a blessedly short period of pushing, during which Esther insisted on squatting. I knelt next to her and watched as the translucent silver sac preceded the head.

"The caul," Annie whispered. "I've never seen it."

"Yes."

I gently tore the membrane away from the face and caught the wriggling dusky-skinned body as it—he—slid out. The newborn gave a healthy cry. I glanced at the clock, which read four eighteen. "Thee has a baby boy, Esther."

A wide smile spread across her face. "My husband will be wildly happy."

I tied and cut the cord, wiped down the little fellow, and swaddled him. Annie helped Esther up onto the bed. Within five minutes she'd delivered the afterbirth and was holding her son, a look of wonder on her face. Annie headed out to summon Akwasi, while I tidied up the room and put away our supplies.

"Rose, I feel in love." When she stroked the baby's cheek with her finger, he turned his head toward her touch in the rooting reaction of all newborns. "I didn't expect this."

"It's as it should be, Esther."

By five o'clock Annie and I stood on the front walk, having left a delighted father with a healthy baby and mother all nestled in the bed together. The little boy had had his first nursing and already seemed expert at it.

"Wouldn't it be nice if all births were that easy?" Annie asked.

"Indeed."

"And to see a baby born in the sac of waters was remarkable."

"Isn't it? Traditional cultures regarded being born in an intact bag as an omen that the baby would grow into a seer—or a healer." Orpha believed the same. She'd told me I had been born in the caul, and that I had the gift of seeing. I covered an unavoidable yawn. "I'm sorry."

She peered into my face. "Rose, you look exhausted. You weren't at a birth last night, too, were you?"

I hadn't had a chance to tell her about Orpha, so I did. "She went peacefully, Annie. And now we carry on her work."

"I'm sorry, Rose." She stroked my arm. "I know how close you were to her."

"Thank thee. I was."

"To change the subject for a moment, if I may, my brother is all agitated about being questioned by the police. He knows it's the right thing to do, but he's not happy about it."

"They probably don't have a single French Canadian on the force, am I right?" I asked.

"They don't. We encounter a big dose of prejudice against us simply because of where we were born."

"I hope things will change with time. We're all immigrants, after all. None of us is originally from this continent, except the Indians." I'd gotten to know a Wampanoag midwife last fall on Cape Cod and quite enjoyed her company. I'd even accompanied her to a birth and picked up a few tips. "One doesn't encounter them here in Amesbury despite the name of the highest hill in town."

"I've wondered about Powow Hill and the Powow River. Maybe it's history someone will uncover one day. But back to Pierrot. Apparently, they kept pressing him about what he saw. The thing is, Rose, he doesn't see well."

"Oh?"

"He's terribly myopic but refuses to wear spectacles."

I touched my own glasses. "That must hamper him in his life."

"It does. He didn't finish school. Being a night watchman is one of the only jobs he can handle."

"Why does he refuse help with his vision?"

"He says men will take him for a sissy if he wears glasses." Annie shook her head. "Isn't that the silliest thing?"

It was. But Pete's bad vision might also mean he couldn't positively identify Zeb as the person he saw running. This was a good thing. A very good thing.

A snowflake fell on my nose. I glanced up to see more floating down, lazy and soft. "We'd better get ourselves home before this turns into a storm."

"Go get some rest, Rose." She gave me a quick hug and bustled off down toward Main Street.

I trudged up the hill in the opposite direction. The Ayensu family had skirted death, as did any birthing woman. They had come out of it more than intact. If only the same could happen for our town, with a killer behind bars and its residents safe to go about their lives.

TWENTY-ONE

I AWOKE THE NEXT MORNING to a world covered in white. And a man bringing me coffee in bed.

"Good morning, my lovely wife. Did you get enough sleep?" He set the coffee on the small table by the bed and perched next to me with a smile.

"What time is it?" I pushed up to sitting and rubbed my eyes.

"Seven thirty."

I blinked. "Did I just sleep for twelve hours?" After we'd eaten a simple supper of leftover stew and bread last evening, I hadn't been able to keep my eyes open.

"You did, my dear. And well needed the rest, I expect."

"Apparently. Grief is exhausting, although I've been so busy since Orpha passed, I think I've been burying it, not allowing it to rise up and overtake me." I sipped the milky coffee. "This is heaven, husband. I thank thee."

He smoothed back a lock of my hair. "What do you have planned for this day?"

"Let's see." I frowned, picturing my schedule. "It's Sixth Day. I have a full morning of prenatal visits, and I'll stop by Esther's this afternoon to check on her baby. Oh, and I'll visit Alma to find out about any funeral arrangements. Maybe my new garments will be ready, as well."

"Sounds busy. Shall we eat at the Grand Hotel tonight? We'll have a delicious dinner, and neither of us will have to cook."

"That would be wonderful." I gazed at him. "Thee is all dressed and ready to go. Would thee ever consider opening an office here in Amesbury instead of having to go across the bridge every day? I know we've discussed it before, but it seems that now would be a good time."

He touched my nose. "I have an appointment this very afternoon to look at a possible space. Did you read my mind?" He laughed. "I want to be closer by after the baby comes."

"I would like knowing thee was nearer to hand. Thee could come home for a midday meal together, too."

75

"Exactly. For now, I'd better be off." He kissed my lips, then stood. "I expect you're going to add sleuthing on top of all your other tasks today."

"I might, just a little."

"You'll be careful, dear Rosie. Please?"

I extended my hand. "Only if I get another kiss before thee leaves."

The kiss having been accomplished to our mutual satisfaction, he was gone. I sat in bed with my coffee, feeling much pampered and refreshed.

Our lovely bedroom was at the back of the house. The neighboring house was situated far enough down the hill that we had no need to draw the shades at night. I watched through the window as sunlight played with snow-coated branches, making the tall sugar maple outside sparkle with diamond-studded fur. When a squirrel alit on a branch, the white stuff slid off. March snows weren't the kind to stick around and accumulate.

As we approached the spring equinox, the days were long enough to melt snow not long after it fell. My list of tasks, as David put it, was also long. I should rouse myself and get started on it. But first I ran my mind's eye down the notes I'd begun yesterday morning. I could add Pete Beaumont's myopia to it, and William's financial troubles. Prudence's drinking problem might play a role, too, although I couldn't think of what.

A visit to Kevin might be in order after I'd finished with my clients, and a talk with Wilson. And seeing Alma, where reminders of Orpha would be everywhere.

I finally took a moment to think back on my many memories of my mentor. Her taking both my hands, gazing into my face, and agreeing to take me on as her apprentice. I'd summoned my courage and asked her after I had helped out at my niece Betsy's birth ten years ago, a birth Orpha had assisted my sister with. The day when Orpha had said I was ready to attend births on my own and soon after had offered me her own practice, declaring she was too old to continue staying up all night with laboring women. The countless times I'd gone to her for counsel about difficult pregnancies, techniques for breech and twin births, solace after a newborn had died at only minutes or hours old. And for her wisdom when I was on the track of a murderer. Rather than tell me what to do, she would ask me questions until the answer arose.

I heard her voice in my head now. "I have every confidence in you, Rose."

I'd better get on with it, then.

TWENTY-TWO

I WAS BUSY WITH PAPERWORK IN MY OFFICE at half past eight when I glanced up at a knock. I wasn't expecting my first client until nine, but two women stood outside, and I could see through the lace curtain that one was my blind friend Jeanette Papka. Her hand was tucked through the elbow of Frannie Eisenman, a woman I'd met through the Amesbury Woman Suffrage Association a couple of years ago. I had a pang, remembering my aunt's teenage ward, also named Frannie, who had been murdered last fall. I pulled the door open.

"Jeanette? How nice to see thee, and Frannie, too. Please come in."

I shut the door after them, wondering what they'd come about. Frannie's frizzed dark hair was shot through with silver. I'd delivered her grandbaby a year and a half ago. She was unlikely to be pregnant. I'd caught Jeanette's very large son Owen at his birth last Tenth Month and hoped she wasn't carrying another baby so soon.

"Please sit here, Jeanette." I led her to my chair. "Frannie, does thee mind the chaise?" I pulled out a stool from the corner and perched on it. "What can I help with today? Is either of thee—?"

Jeanette threw her head back and laughed. "Good heavens, no, Rose. Neither of us is pregnant."

Frannie snorted. "I went through the change a decade ago, thank goodness."

"And my boy is such a lusty nursling, I can't imagine my body would think it was time to make another baby already." Jeanette patted her bosom with a grin. "Do you know he weighs twenty-five pounds at five months?" She shook her head.

"He was thirteen pounds at birth, and long, to boot," I said.

"Yes, he certainly was." Jeanette nodded. Her second labor and birth had gone surprisingly easily, despite the baby's remarkable size. "Listen, Rose. Frannie here heard something interesting, and I convinced her we should come straightaway and tell you."

"You have information, too, Jeanette," Frannie said.

"Yes, I might."

I glanced from one to the other. "Is it about the murder?"

"I think so," Frannie replied. "I have a kitchen girl, but she only comes twice a week, as it's only Mr. Eisenman and me at home now. She mainly does for Mr. Bailey."

"Which Bailey?" I asked.

"Mr. Ned Bailey."

Ah. I waited for her to go on, then thought of a question. "Is Ned married?" He hadn't been when he was pestering me to step out with him, but his circumstances might have changed.

"No," Frannie replied. "The man doesn't have much luck with the ladies. He lives alone."

"I've met him," Jeanette said. "I'm not surprised he's still a bachelor despite being well up in his thirties. He's like an overeager puppy, that one."

I smothered a laugh. It was an apt description for Ned.

"In any event," Frannie began, "my girl said she spied Mr. Bailey hiding something in his bureau the morning the poor visitor's death was reported."

"It was Tuesday," Jeanette offered.

"Yes." Frannie nodded. "He went off to the Opening. Later she was putting away his clean laundry, and what did she find? A gun. A gun, I tell you! In his unmentionables drawer."

I stared. Lighthearted Ned? He didn't seem like a killer to me. On the other hand, he had cast a peculiar look at me after I'd mentioned hearing about his uncle's plans being stolen.

Jeanette nodded sagely. She'd clearly heard the story.

"Goodness. Is she willing to speak to the police?" I asked Frannie.

"I doubt it. She's pretty much fresh off the boat from Greece, and she doesn't trust anyone in uniform. I think someone in her family was maltreated by either the police or the military."

"Would thee be willing to report it?" I asked Frannie.

She wrinkled her nose. "I'd have to give them her name, and then she'd quit on me, I'm sure of it."

I suspected this was very likely in both cases.

"Can't you find some way to tell your detective buddy, Rose?" Jeanette asked. "I mean, a way not involving Frannie's girl?"

"I can try. I assume the girl left the gun there."

"Naturally," Frannie said. "She was in quite a tizzy about even seeing it. She never would have touched it."

The clock was inching closer to nine o'clock, when my first pregnant lady was due to arrive. "I'm sorry, but I have a client coming in ten minutes. Jeanette, did thee say thee had information to share, too?"

"Perhaps. I haven't yet returned to my live interpreting job at the court, but a lawyer I know brought me a paper yesterday to translate into Polish along with another document in French he needed put into English. We chatted a bit, and he said the Parry factory is in dire straits."

"I heard something about Parry having financial problems, too," I said.

"He also mentioned Zebulon Weed," Jeanette continued. "He's a fellow Quaker, isn't he?"

My heart sank. "Yes. What did he know about Zeb?"

"He's representing young Zebulon."

I stared at her. "Was Zeb arrested yesterday?"

"I don't believe so, but the senior Weed seemed to think his son needed a lawyer."

And maybe he did.

TWENTY-THREE

I DIDN'T GET TO THE POLICE STATION until half past one. Making a telephone call to Kevin about Ned's gun would be a very bad idea. This was a talk we needed to have in person. And we hadn't spoken about the murder since Third Day, the day after it happened.

A dazzling sun shone on the snow, which was melting fast, and the air smelled fresh and clean. After I popped in to check on Esther and baby—both blessedly thriving—I walked into town rather than cycling through the slush. A robin hopped on a bare-limbed oak. A squirrel leaping onto a branch in an elm overhead plopped a clump of wet snow squarely on my bonnet. The wheel of a wide dray pulled by a tired-looking gray mare dipped through a puddle and splashed me. My shoes and hems were soaked through by the time I arrived at the station. The fresh-faced young man usually behind the counter had been replaced by a florid older officer with what looked like a permanent scowl etched onto his face.

I greeted him with a smile, anyway. "I'd like to speak with Kevin Donovan, if thee pleases."

"Not here."

"When does thee expect him back?"

"Don't know." He nearly barked the words.

I erased the smile from my face and stood up to my full height. "Please inform him Mrs. Rose Dodge needs to speak with him at his earliest convenience."

He gave one slow nod and didn't write down my name. I suppressed a sigh at this unhelpful man's lack of response. Weren't police officers public servants with an obligation to help the citizens of our fair town? This one must have forgotten the service part of his training. Was it that he disrespected my faith, which was always revealed by my speech and bonnet? Or maybe this was how he treated all females. Perhaps he thought my gender had no place inquiring into police business.

I turned toward the door but stepped out of the way when it opened. A young officer tugged on a middle-aged woman, holding her upper arm in a tight grip.

"Come along now, Mrs. Weed," he said. "You know I've got to charge you."

My jaw dropped as I took a second look. This was indeed Prudence Weed, Zeb's mother. She wasn't wearing a bonnet over curly graying hair escaping its hairpins. Her round face was flushed, her eyes bright and bloodshot, and her coat flapped open. I brought my hand to my mouth.

"Another drunk and disorderly for her?" asked the cross-tempered man behind the counter.

"Yes, sir," the younger fellow said. "Found her on a bench singing at the top of her lungs."

"It's not a crime to sing in public," Prudence protested with slurred diction.

"It is when you're tippling out of a bottle of hooch at the same time." Her escort pulled a pint bottle out of his pocket. Only half an inch of an amber liquor remained in the bottom. "And when proper ladies are giving you a wide berth as they pass."

The older officer cocked his thumb toward the door to the back. "Lock her up. I'll call the husband." His voice was tired, as if he'd been through this routine before, which he no doubt had.

"I can tell the Weeds she's here," I offered.

Prudence gazed at me as if she'd only now seen me. "Well, hello there, Rose. Did they lock thee up, too? Did thee just get freed?" She gave me a sloppy smile.

I inwardly recoiled from the stench of alcohol on her breath. "No, Prudence." I struggled with what to say next. Scolding her for being drunk before two o'clock in the afternoon would be pointless and cruel. Wishing her a lovely day would be silly. Who enjoyed time in a jail cell? Asking her why she drank wasn't the right question, either, at least not here and now. But it gave me an idea.

"Instead of calling her family, might I accompany Prudence to her cell and help get her settled?" I asked. I'd visited others in jail in earlier years, but never a woman. "We attend the same church."

The two men exchanged a glance. "That'd be fine," the older one said. "The matron isn't present right now."

From a previous case, I knew the department employed only one woman, whose primary role was to watch over female prisoners.

"I thank thee." I followed the younger officer and Prudence into the back, turning into the holding area after he unlocked the heavy door. The cell they reserved for women was the back one of the three, for privacy, I supposed. Blessedly the men's cells were unoccupied, or Prudence might have been subjected to a dose of verbal abuse.

After the officer unlocked the door, it creaked as it opened. Inside sat a cot with a ratty gray blanket, a small washstand with a chipped pitcher and basin, and a wastes bucket smelling as if it had not been recently scrubbed. The small barred window hadn't had a cleaning lately, either.

Prudence plodded in and sank onto the cot with a groan.

The officer looked from her to me. "I ought to lock her in, but if you want to stay and visit a bit, suit yourself. She's not dangerous. Shut the door when you leave, and let me or my buddy out there know."

"I thank thee."

"She's not exactly a flight risk in her condition." He gave a little toss of his head and disappeared back down the hall.

Prudence gave me a hopeful look. "Did thee bring me something to eat? I am famished of a sudden."

"I'm sorry, no. Perhaps I can fetch something and bring it back." There was nowhere to sit except next to her on the questionable blanket. A year ago I would have perched there. Now, carrying a child, I didn't dare. Who knew what vermin lurked in the cloth or on the thin mattress under it?

"Never thee mind." She mustered a wan smile. "My husband will release me soon enough, I daresay. Or maybe young Zeb will. He's such a good boy."

"He is. And a good husband to Faith."

She bowed her head, staring at her clasped hands. She looked up at me. "Rose, why does my weakness keep getting the better of me? Every morning I resolve not to imbibe, not ever again. But look at me. This is the third time I've been tossed in the clink—in broad daylight." Her voice rose and ended in a pitiful sob.

I laid my hand on her shoulder. "I don't know why, Prudence. Some are susceptible to overeating, thinking food will assuage their pain. Others fall prey to laudanum or other opiates. Thee clearly has a weakness for hard spirits. Complete abstention would be thy only cure."

"I know," she murmured, her voice barely above a whisper, as her shoulders sank. "Thee remembers when we lost poor Isaiah in the Great Fire?"

"Of course. It was a terrible day." Two years ago, the disastrous fire that nearly destroyed Amesbury's carriage industry also took the lives of some of its workers. Zeb's younger brother Isaiah, who'd been stepping out with Annie, had been one of the victims.

"The drink helps me forget the pain of losing him." She studied her hands. "If I stopped imbibing, I'd have to face my anguish square on. And more. Whiskey is like an old, comfortable friend to me."

I nodded. I'd heard this reaction from others who struggled with their emotions, including my brother-in-law Frederick. For a time, missing my late sister, he'd drowned his sorrow in drink—to the detriment of his children—until he'd met Winnie. Blessedly, I'd seen no further evidence of his drinking since then.

"Wouldn't thee like to resume thy music?" I asked. "Teaching and performing?"

She wagged her head with a sorrowful look. "Rose, that ship has sailed."

I supposed it had. "Does thee sometimes drink in public late at night?"

"Thee heard," she finally said, gazing down again.

"I don't know if I have." I tucked my skirts under me and squatted next to the cot, bringing my face level with hers. "Tell me."

"When the Canadian was killed." She covered her mouth with her hand, blue eyes wide above it.

I waited. Silence was normally my friend. Not now. "And?"

"I was there." At the creak of the jail area door, Prudence clamped her mouth shut.

Kevin strode in. "Heard you wanted to talk with me, Miss . . ." His voice trailed off when he spied me inside the cell with Prudence. To his credit, he didn't glare at her, instead giving her a kindly look. "Ah, Mrs. Weed. Back for another visit, I see."

If I were one to curse, I would do so now. She'd been about to tell me something important, her words flowing almost as fast as the water in the Powow River. But the gate on that millrace had just clanged shut.

TWENTY-FOUR

"I THINK PRUDENCE SAW SOMETHING the night of the murder," I told Kevin in his office a few minutes later. "She was about to tell me when thee walked in."

"More's the pity. I'll have a little chat with her before she leaves."

"Good."

"But Mrs. Weed landing back in the lockup isn't why you were looking for me." He tilted his head and tented his fingers.

"No." I considered how to phrase the information about the gun. If I told him, Frannie's girl would have to be involved. I had no way to get around Kevin needing to speak with her. I let out a sigh. It was unavoidable. "Apparently Ned Bailey has a gun in his bureau at home. The girl who works for him saw him hurrying to hide something the morning after the murder."

"What?" Kevin slammed his hand on the table.

"She later was putting away his clean laundry and saw the gun." I didn't need to tell Kevin it was in with his undergarments. He would only be embarrassed.

"How in the devil's name did you learn this?" he asked.

"Thee needn't bring Lucifer into the matter, Kevin."

"I apologize, Miss Rose. You're right." He chuckled. "You always keep me on the straight and narrow, as it were. Now, about this information. Who is this mysterious girl?"

"I have an acquaintance named Mrs. Frannie Eisenman. The girl who helps in her kitchen primarily works for Ned. Frannie told me this morning." I held up my hand when he began to speak. "I didn't get the girl's name. Frannie said she's a recent immigrant from Greece and is terrified of police."

"Eisenman, you say?" He scribbled on a notepad.

"Yes, with one *n* at the end. She lives down near the beginning of Maple Street, not far from the Friends Meetinghouse."

"Duly noted."

"Is thee going to need to talk with the girl?" I asked.

"If I do, I'll be gentle, have no fear. But it's possible going straight to the source will be more effective."

85

"To Ned. Good idea. If this gun was the murder weapon, why would he have it in his possession if he didn't use it?"

He nodded slowly. "I suppose he could have come across it the next morning wherever the killer dropped it. But he should have brought it directly to us, not secret it away in his own home. I confess this case continues to confound me. I could use a break in it."

"Thee isn't holding Zeb Weed."

"I have no evidence against him. And he won't tell me a blasted thing, either."

"How about the plans that were taken?" I asked. "Has thee learned what they were?"

"Mr. Bailey the elder said they were for some kind of new model."

"Who had the opportunity to steal them?"

He frowned. "He couldn't remember where he'd left them. I think he's going soft in the head, frankly. But I do know Mr. Ned Bailey took both those Canadians to visit his uncle the evening before the murder."

"Didn't I tell thee so?"

"You quite possibly might have."

I cocked my head, thinking. "Kevin, I don't think I've had the chance to tell thee what Ned told me the next day about his own plans. Have I?"

"No, you have not." He looked exasperated. "Out with it, Miss Rose."

He must be feeling frustrated with the lack of progress. "He said he wants to put a motor in a carriage body and make a vehicle that moves by its own power. He called it a motorcar. The missing plans might be for exactly that."

"A motorcar?" He squinted at me. "That's crazy."

"Maybe, or perhaps it's the future. I just realized I'd never shared that with thee. Although Ned made it sound like he had drawn up the plans, not his uncle."

"Be that as it may," Kevin said. "I also haven't gotten anywhere with Mr. Parry."

"How about with Luthera?" I asked. "Has thee determined her whereabouts the night of the murder?"

"Mrs. Harrington? Have you lost your senses, Miss Rose?"

"Not at all. I can think of a number of reasons a wife might have to extinguish her husband's life."

"True enough. The answer is no, I haven't. Yet." He stood and clapped his hat on his head. "But first I have to see a man about a gun."

I pushed up to standing. Kevin took a second look at me.

"I say, Miss Rose. I hope this isn't overly forward of me to say, but I'd venture a guess you are in the blessed way. Am I right?"

I laughed. "If by that thee means am I pregnant? Yes, I am. David and I have been well blessed and will have a baby of our own this summer."

Kevin beamed. "That's splendid news. I'll tell my Emmaline tonight, if I may. She'll be thrilled for you."

"Please do tell her."

"You'd best not be doing any more assisting in this case. I mean, I thank you for the information you bring me, but you have a wee bun in the oven to protect."

"I promise not to do anything to endanger myself or the foetus, Kevin." This was a promise I intended to keep.

TWENTY-FIVE

I TRUDGED TO ALMA'S HOUSE, my steps growing heavier the closer I got. My grief at losing Orpha had been suppressed by Esther's birth and the investigation. It now flooded back in. I could only imagine how Alma was feeling. Still, my dress became tighter by the hour, it seemed. Alma had telephoned this morning saying my new garments were ready. It would be an enormous relief not to have a constriction around my waist.

Alma pulled open the door and welcomed me in.

"How is thee?" I asked her.

"I'm sad. Having work to do helps. And you?"

"The same." I gazed at Orpha's rocking chair in the parlor where we stood, and my eyes filled. I looked away, but the doorway beyond led to her bedroom. Her death room. "Is she still . . . ?" I couldn't finish.

"No. The Rogers funeral parlor men came yesterday. And speaking of funerals, we're going to hold the service tomorrow afternoon at the Main Street Congregational Church. We'll gather here afterward. You'll come, won't you?"

"I wouldn't miss it. What time?"

"The funeral will be at two o'clock," she said. "Dr. Chatigny has been a great help."

"I'm glad. Is thy father coming?"

She cast her eyes upward for a moment. "Yes, my parents will arrive tonight. How someone as good as Nana produced a difficult man like him is beyond me. My husband is hurrying back with the girls, too, which will help. Somehow Mr. Latting gets along better with Father than I do."

"Good. May I bring food for the gathering?"

"No, don't trouble yourself. The good Congregational ladies are handling refreshments, for which I am grateful." She gestured toward the stairs. "Shall we?"

I followed her up to her sewing room and exclaimed at the two loose dresses hanging ready for me. "Thee is a miracle worker."

She'd found the lawn in a plain dusky green, and the other was of

Quaker gray, as we liked to call it, but in a polished cotton. The fabric was shirred into tiny pleats at the shoulders and flowed down in loose folds from there, front and back.

"They are identical except for cloth and color," Alma said. "Try one on, and I'll see if I have to make any adjustments. They fasten down the front, and I used hooks and eyes instead of buttons. I had a dress like this when I was nursing my girlies. Hooks and eyes made it much easier to open the front one-handed and feed them."

"I hadn't thought of that aspect." Sewing on hooks and eyes was indeed a brilliant idea. I unfastened the buttons at my waist. "Oh, that's better. Alma, if there are any alterations, thee will have to do them on the spot. I plan to wear one of these home." I'd be glad to get out of my wet hems.

Alma laughed and pointed at the Oriental screen she provided for modesty. I emerged in the gray version a minute later. Its slightly heavier cotton would be warmer. She looked at me, felt the shoulders, and turned me to face away.

"Yes, I think it's perfect, and the length is, too. Do you agree?"

"I do." It fell to my ankles but didn't sweep the floor. I turned around again, running my hands down the front and sides. "You added pockets. I like that."

"I try to provide all my ladies with pockets if they want them. You, I didn't ask, knowing what a practical person you are. Believe me, when you're carrying a baby around, it helps to have somewhere to stash a handkerchief or a teether."

"I'm glad."

"Let me wrap up the green one and the dress you wore here." Alma headed to a wide roll of paper in the corner.

"Can thee possibly wrap them separately? The slush out there drenched my hems as I walked."

"Certainly." As she worked, she shook her head. "You know, the lady I told you about, the one I sold the widow's dress to?"

"Luthera Harrington."

"Yes, her. I'd included a pocket in the black dress, but she was unhappy about it. She claimed she would never have a use for one and instructed me to stitch it closed."

"Truly?" I asked.

"Yes."

"She does seem like someone who has always had others to make her life easier." I pictured her privileged airs. "Maybe she can't conceive of anything so practical as a pocket."

"It might have come in handy if she'd wanted to hide the gun she shot her husband with."

I stared at Alma.

"Well, you know." She handed me my packages. "In the Pinkerton novel I read, the wife was the first suspect."

TWENTY-SIX

As GEORGIA'S HOME ON POWOW STREET was only two blocks from Alma's, I decided to stop by in case I could speak to Wilson. I had a little pang because of my promise to Kevin, but what harm could come of a brief conversation with the driver if I were in the company of a friend?

"Rose, good afternoon," Georgia Clarke said as her driver helped her down from the carriage in the covered *porte cochere* attached to her house.

This was a stroke of luck.

"Do you have any news?" she whispered.

"Hello, Georgia. No, I don't, but I actually wondered if I could have a word with Wilson."

Wilson, his back to us, seemed to freeze at hearing me say his name.

"Whatever you need," Georgia said. "Wilson?"

He clicked shut the door of the carriage, then turned slowly. His neat black suit and driving cap had the look of a uniform. He was clean-shaven, and intelligent gray eyes regarded me from under bushy eyebrows already going white. His build was trim, his spine straight, his expression wary.

I wondered what he thought he had to fear from me.

"Yes, Mrs. Clarke?" he asked.

"This is my friend Mrs. Dodge. She'd like to speak with you for a moment."

"Very well, ma'am. Shall I put up Silver first?" He gestured toward the horse.

Georgia gave me an inquiring glance.

"This shouldn't take long," I said.

"I need to move to the front, Mrs. Dodge," Wilson said.

"Please," I replied.

Wilson stepped toward the aptly named steed.

"Is Luthera around?" I asked Georgia.

"No, she's out with the carriage doings. I don't expect her back until this evening."

Good.

A white-clad nursemaid stepped into the doorway of the home holding a red-faced Rosie, who extended her arms toward Georgia and wailed for her mother.

Georgia laughed. "Excuse me, Rose. Your namesake wants her mama." She patted her bosom and leaned toward me, murmuring, "She still wants her milkie a few times a day. I know she's almost two, but I don't mind. She's my last baby."

"Go then," I said, smiling.

"Are you headed home from here?" she asked me.

"Yes."

"Wilson, please drive Mrs. Dodge to her house when you're done talking. She'll direct you."

"Yes, ma'am." Wilson touched the brim of his cap.

"I thank thee, Georgia." My feet were chilled from getting wet earlier, and a cold breeze had blown up, too. A ride would be lovely. I moved closer to Wilson. "I'm pleased to make thy acquaintance, Wilson. Has thee worked for Georgia long?"

"Yes, ma'am. I've been with Mr. Clarke's family since I was a lad." He smoothed the neck of the horse, whose light gray coat was indeed nearly silver.

"I see. I wondered if thee might be able to tell me what time thee drove Luthera Harrington home on Second Day evening this week. What thee calls Monday," I hastened to add.

He gazed directly at me for the first time. His lips rounded, as if he was about to ask "Why?" Instead, he closed his mouth and nodded. "Yes, ma'am. It was nearly midnight."

"That's late. Does thee live here on the property?"

"I have quarters in the carriage house, ma'am." He glanced toward the back, where a sizeable two-story carriage house stood, with trim and paint to match the main house.

"Where did thee pick up Luthera, if I may ask?"

"Why, in front of the opera house, ma'am. It's where the evening's festivities were held."

"Was she alone?"

He blinked, and the corners of his mouth turned down. "Of course not, ma'am. That would be unseemly for a lady. Mr. Clarke escorted her."

"I see. Did she seem flustered or . . . ?" I let my voice trail off. I couldn't very well ask if she'd had blood on her.

"I'm sure I wouldn't know, ma'am."

Or didn't want to say, more likely. "Well, I thank thee for this information."

"Would you like to return home now, Mrs. Dodge?" His tone sounded like he would like to be rid of me, even if I wasn't ready to go.

But I was out of questions for now. And I had new things to ponder.

"Yes, please."

TWENTY-SEVEN

DAVID AND I SAT AT A TABLE NEXT TO A WINDOW that evening in the Grand Hotel, which perched atop Whittier Hill, one of the highest points in Amesbury. The lights of the town twinkled in the distance below. The clink of silver on china and a room full of murmured conversations surrounded us.

I gazed at what remained of my chicken cutlet, which had been delicately flavored with herbs and lemon. A final morsel of mashed potatoes and one last asparagus spear, imported from somewhere south of here, still awaited me. Around here the tasty shoots didn't come up until mid-May. Across from me, my husband popped in the last bite of his roast beef, which had been served with a mushroom sauce and potato croquettes. We'd managed not to discuss the murder once during dinner.

"I am nearly full to the brim," I said. "But not quite." I cut a piece of asparagus and savored it.

"This is a nice break, isn't it?" David sipped from his red wine.

"It certainly is. Thank thee for suggesting it."

"And you look lovely in your new frock, my dear."

"Thank thee." I smiled at him. For our outing, I'd changed into the green dress, which was plain and pretty at the same time. I felt vain liking that it complemented my coloring, but even Friends want to look nice for their dearly beloved. What with the bloom of pregnancy on my cheeks, I hadn't needed to use any "Quaker rouge," the rub of a mullein leaf that pinkened skin in a pleasant way. "This style is ever so much more comfortable."

"And if you are at ease, the baby will be as well, isn't that right?"

"I believe so." I thought of what Esther had said about Akwasi being overjoyed at having a baby boy. "David, does thee hope very much for a son?" I resettled my spectacles, which had a habit of slipping down my nose.

"Rose, don't you know me by now? A son would make me happy, but so will a daughter. All I care about is you and the baby making it through in good health. I'm not the archaic type of man like the new father you told me about last year, who wouldn't even acknowledge his newborn daughter after her twin brother died."

"Because all he wanted was a son," I said, remembering.

"Our child will be perfect, regardless of its sex."

"We are in agreement." I smiled at him.

"I have some news. I agreed to let offices on Market Street today."

I clapped my hands. "That's wonderful. I'm so glad, dear David."

"As am I. It's near the square, and in the same building as Dr. Norton, the homeopathist. I'll switch my attending privileges to the Methodist Hospital a little farther out on Market next month."

"Bravo." I gazed out at the darkness. Despite the beauty of the evening, it brought to mind the night of Justice's murder. Luthera hadn't left the opera house until midnight, but she'd been with Robert Clarke. Being escorted home did not clear her of the murder, though. She could have left the festivities earlier, shot her husband, and returned. For that matter, so could have Ned or William. Were Kevin and his men asking all who had been present their whereabouts and what they'd seen? I hoped so.

"A penny for your thoughts, my dear?" David asked gently. "Or maybe I needn't pay. I wager you're thinking about"—he glanced around and lowered his voice to a murmur—"this week's events."

"Thee knows me too well. I spoke with Kevin this afternoon. He doesn't seem to be making much progress." I glanced up as a couple approached us. When I saw it was Jonathan Sherwood with a pleasant-looking woman, I smiled.

"Good evening, Jonathan," I said. "Has thee met my husband, David Dodge? David, this is Jonathan Sherwood of Lowell's Boat Shop. He also sits on the Board of Trade."

David rose and the men shook hands.

"This is my wife, Amy," Jonathan said. "Amy, midwife Rose Dodge."

We exchanged pleasantries. "Did thee enjoy thy meal?" I asked her.

"Very much," Amy said.

Jonathan nodded his agreement.

"I had an excellent older midwife here in town for our son's birth ten years ago," she said. "Do you know Mrs. Perkins, Mrs. Dodge?"

I nodded once even as my smile slipped away and grief flooded me again. "Orpha was my teacher, and I took over her practice. I'm sad to say she passed away this week."

"I'm very sorry to hear this," Amy said.

"As am I," Jonathan added. "She provided superb care for Amy and our baby."

"Her funeral is tomorrow afternoon at two, at Main Street Congregational," I told them.

"Thank you." He glanced at his wife, who bobbed her head. "I expect we'll see you there."

Here in front of me was someone who doubtless was at the opera house Second Day night. I didn't want to waste this opportunity. "Jonathan, did thee attend the Spring Opening festivities Monday evening?"

He looked over the top of his spectacles at me. He knew I had been involved in an investigation last year after I'd had to inform a victim's husband — someone Jonathan supervised — of his wife's death.

"Yes, I was," he finally said.

I reconsidered. This was not the time or place to be asking him questions about Luthera's — or anyone's — whereabouts during the event.

"May I stop by the boat shop tomorrow? I have a question or two for thee."

"Please. I'll be there all morning." He tucked Amy's hand through his elbow.

"I thank thee. It was very nice to meet thee, Amy."

"Likewise, Mrs. Dodge." She smiled. "So far we have but the one child, but should I have need of a midwife again, I will seek you out."

"Please do."

The menfolk shook hands again and the Sherwoods made their way toward the door. Before they reached it, an usher escorted the green-eyed man from the Board of Trade meeting — the Brazilian, apparently — to a small table set for one.

David sat. "Doing a little sleuthing, I see."

"Just a little. The thing is, the key has to be what happened during the banquet the night of the murder. Someone persuaded Justice Harrington to leave and then shot him in the alley. Did he or she then return to the event as if nothing had happened or go home?"

"You think Mr. Sherwood might have seen something to provide an answer." He reached over and took my hand.

"He's an ethical and observant man with a good memory. If he noticed something suspicious, he'll tell me."

"And you, my dear wife, will take the information to the police rather than acting on it."

I squeezed his hand. "I will."

TWENTY-EIGHT

AFTER BREAKFAST WITH DAVID, I sent him along on his morning work. I donned my split cycling skirt, which luckily was roomier around the waist than my regular dresses, and set out on my steel steed to speak with Jonathan Sherwood. It was after nine o'clock when I turned onto Main Street and coasted down the hill. The day before had been sunny enough to melt away the slush. Patches of snow remained only in north-facing shaded spots.

As I pedaled past Patten's Pond, I spied a tall man leaning against a tree, staring into the water. I braked to a stop.

"Zeb?" I called.

He turned and gave a half-hearted wave.

I wheeled the bicycle off the road and leaned it on the tree. I resettled my bonnet, which was always flying akilter from the wind created by riding, and took a closer look at him. His face was gaunt, and the dark smudges under his eyes made him look far older than his twenty-one years.

"Zeb," I kept my voice gentle. "What's the matter?"

He waited while the river-bound trolley clattered by, still pulled by horses. "Rose, other than when my brother died, this has been the worst week of my life."

"Tell me." I waited but got only silence in return. "Truly, it can help to unburden cares onto someone who loves thee."

He folded his arms and gazed across the pond at the massive four-story Locke & Jewell carriage factory. "Very well. I've finally attained a position of some responsibility. I'm off the factory floor and meeting the carriage-buying public. I thought all was well. I thought Faith and I could start a family soon. But then I hear my employer is having financial troubles. I'm questioned as a suspicious person in a murder investigation. My own mother is a sad embarrassment, the laughingstock of the town. Even Faith is giving me odd looks. What am I to do?"

"Look at me, dear nephew." I waited until he did. "Has thee done anything wrong? Any act illegal or unethical?"

"I never would." He shook his head, hard.

"I didn't think so. Then let us take these concerns one at a time. William Parry first. If his business goes under, thee will find employment elsewhere. Thee is gaining a reputation as a well-spoken, intelligent, informed salesman. I daresay Robert Clarke would welcome thee, or the Bailey business."

"Maybe." He stared at the ground.

I continued. "And we both know their products are of a higher quality."

"That is most certainly true."

"As for thy mother, I spoke with her yesterday after she was jailed."

He raised his shoulders in a wince.

"She needs to stop drinking entirely," I said in a gentle voice, "but the impulse has to come from her."

"I know, Rose."

"Would that she could go to a residence like a tuberculosis sanitarium, but one instead designed to help the recovery of those addicted to spirits. There is the Martha Washington Home in Chicago, a rehabilitation center only for women, and the New York Inebriate Asylum. I also know of several Keeley Institutes, but their injections of bichloride of gold seem like a questionable cure."

"Either way, we'd have to get her to agree to go. At least my father got her home yesterday." Zeb shook his head. "I don't even know where she finds the stuff."

"I understand. Now, about the murder. I'm working with the police on the matter. It will help if thee tells me everything, every detail, about Second Day evening. What thee saw, what thee heard."

"I told them, Kevin and his lackeys." He shoved his hands in his pockets.

"Zeb." I got his attention and pointed at my face. "Tell me. Come sit down." I perched on a bench someone had placed near the shore of the pond.

He plopped down next to me, leaning his elbows on his knees. "Mother showed up at the opera house, weaving and slurring. Maybe she'd heard there would be free refreshments of the alcoholic variety, I don't know."

"And?" A red-tailed hawk keened as it circled overhead, with its raptor's high-pitched cry, as if wailing for Prudence's affliction.

"I left to walk her home. William Parry wasn't happy with me, but I told him I would be back."

"What time did you leave?"

He frowned. "I think it was a little after ten. These affairs stretch into the night, and it was the first one of the week. They had musicians playing, and everyone was hobnobbing with great energy."

Which would make it difficult for those inside to hear a pistol shot. "Please think carefully. Were Luthera and Justice Harrington still at the opera house when you left?"

"The Canadians? Yes, I believe so."

"Thee said William was there. How about Ned Bailey?"

He pulled his mouth to the side. "I'm not sure about him."

"When thee escorted thy mother home, did thee see anything suspicious?"

"No, although I heard someone in the dark coughing, as if he was ill."

"Could thee tell it was a man's cough?" I asked. "The tubercular rale can be deep."

"True." He narrowed his eyes. "Perhaps I'm not sure of the sex."

"What time did thee return to the opera house?"

"I . . . wait." He sat up straight and twisted to gaze at me. "On my way back, I thought I heard someone running."

"But thee didn't see anyone running?"

"No."

"Nor a body in the alley."

"No!" His eyes went wide. "I would have reported such a sight immediately."

I thought. "What about when thee rejoined the gathering? Did thee see any of those people I mentioned? Justice, Luthera, William, Ned?"

"I can't help with that. As soon as I reentered, I was cornered by some Brazilian gent I could barely understand. I truly witnessed nothing of import."

"I understand. Did thee tell all of this to the police?"

"I might not have." He tilted his head. "They didn't ask the way you did."

"Don't worry. I will relay what thee told me. Did thee catch the Brazilian's name, by the way?"

"He was a Mr. Amado. I think his first name was something like George, except he said it softer, like *Zhor-zhee*."

"Green eyes?"

"Yes." His own blue eyes widened. "How did thee know?"

"It doesn't matter. Now, go home and tell Faith everything. She loves thee. She will understand."

"I will." Zeb blew out a noisy breath through his lips. "Rose, I thank thee. Will thee pray with me for a moment? I could use God's guidance in thy presence."

"As could I." We two Friends folded our hands in our laps and closed our eyes right there next to the public thoroughfare. Nowhere on this earth was the wrong place for praying. I held Zeb and Faith, Prudence and Kevin, and myself in God's Light. I had faith that justice — the legal kind, as it was too late for the mortal one — would be served, as Way opened.

TWENTY-NINE

IT DIDN'T TAKE LONG to cycle the rest of the way down Main Street to the wide Merrimack River. I continued left along Point Shore on Merrimack Street, which paralleled the water, to Lowell's Boat Shop. Other establishments also made ships and boats next to the river. Lowell's had been in business for nearly a hundred years and had a fine reputation.

A couple of minutes later I sat in Jonathan Sherwood's small office with the din of hammers, saws, and men's voices in the shop only slightly muffled by the door. A different, older woman sat in the front reception area, not the young, attractive one from a year ago.

"How can I help you, Mrs. Dodge?" Jonathan folded his hands on the desk, which held only a ledger book, a neat stack of papers, and a light film of sawdust. "Would it be about the unfortunate death of Mr. Harrington?"

"It would. Last night thee confirmed thy attendance at the Spring Opening gathering on Second Day evening. The night Justice was murdered."

"Isn't the name an irony, though, now we know what happened to him?"

I nodded in acknowledgment.

"But you are here inquiring so as to rightly bring him justice," Jonathan went on. "Yes, I was there, along with what seemed like half the town."

"I would like to understand what thee saw as the evening progressed. In particular, did thee notice when Justice left? Who else might have left the hall at the same time?"

He propped one elbow in his hand and set his chin on the other fist, as if thinking. "Let me see, now. Mrs. Harrington seemed intent on conversing with all the carriage factory owners. She carried on a lengthy conversation with Mr. Parry. I believe she sees herself as the duly appointed representative of her father's company."

"More than her husband, who worked for them?"

"Yes."

"Did thee happen to overhear any of Luthera's and William's words?" I asked.

He pulled a wry grin. "Now I feel like an old fishwife telling tales."

"Sometimes an investigation has exactly that feel. But the police don't always know what's important until they put it all together."

"Very well. I was passing by the two—as well as Parry's partner—on my way to the buffet table when I thought I heard the word 'merge.' Perhaps you've learned Mr. Parry's constant mismanagement has led to some troubles with the financial health of his outfit."

"I have."

"To merge his company with the very successful Montgomery Carriage Company of Ottawa might be a wise step for Parry and an astute one for the northerners."

Did Zeb know of such a plan? "I suppose so, although it might mean William would no longer be the head of the company he founded," I said. "I wonder if Justice agreed about a merging."

"That I couldn't tell you. I did see Mr. Harrington putting his head together with Mr. Ned Bailey for some time early in the soiree, plus another man, a dark-haired foreigner."

I raised my eyebrows. "But thee didn't hear what they talked about?" Had it been about the mysterious plans?

"I didn't."

"Or who the foreigner was?"

He shook his head. "I only glimpsed green eyes, although I think I spied him at the Grand Hotel last night. My fishwife identity has its limits."

I smiled at the image of him as a fishwife for a moment. I remembered the green-eyed man—Amado, according to Zeb—sitting behind Ned and me at the Board of Trade meeting. Maybe he overheard the motorcar idea and approached Ned later about it.

Jonathan added, "I will say the trio looked friendly and possibly excited."

"Does thee know Zebulon Weed, who works for William Parry?"

"Yes, after a fashion. He seems an intelligent young man."

"He is, and he's married to my niece. I'm afraid the police think he might have been involved in the killing."

"But why?" He frowned. "What has he to do with the Harringtons?"

"Nothing, to be sure. One thing I am attempting is to clear his name. Can thee tell me if thee saw him leave the hall or return to it?"

He pulled his mouth to the side. "He did escort a woman out, an older lady who appeared embarrassingly inebriated."

I blew out a breath. "It was his own mother, alas. Does thee remember the time?"

"A bit after ten, I think."

The same as Zeb had said. "What else can thee tell me? Did thee witness Justice leave?" I'd asked him earlier, but he hadn't answered.

"No. Unlike many others, I didn't stay on until late."

I sighed inwardly. *Too bad.*

Jonathan continued. "As you can see, I'm in boat building, not the manufacture of carriages and their component parts. I'm only on the Board of Trade as a representative of this business because the Lowell family doesn't care to become involved in the issues before the town."

"I understand," I said. "Have the police been to ask thee for information about the night of the murder?"

"Not yet. Until now I didn't realize I had any." He clasped his hands and shot a quick look at the clock on the wall, which was about to click over to ten thirty.

A brief knock from the interior of the shop sounded, followed by a young man popping his sawdust-powdered head in. "Mr. Sherwood, we'd like your opinion on the new dory design, sir."

"I'll be there forthwith."

The man touched his cap and shut the door.

"Thee has work to do." I stood. "And I must be on my way. I thank thee greatly for being forthcoming. Please do inform Kevin Donovan of any other details thee might remember."

"I shall, as you deem it important." He also rose. "I hope you will take care in your investigation, Mrs. Dodge. To have an unapprehended killer in our midst is an unsettling thought."

"We are in agreement about that."

THIRTY

I STOOD OUTSIDE THE BOAT SHOP, considering my path. I also rued riding my cycle. The pregnant woman's frequent need to pass water—one I knew well from my clients' reports and was now experiencing for myself—was becoming an increasing problem. If I'd walked here or convinced David to drive me, I could easily hire a conveyance home or even hop on the trolley. But transporting a bicycle at the same time was out of the question.

Perhaps I could leave the steel steed here for the moment. I truly wanted to convey what I'd learned to Kevin, and then I needed to prepare myself, both my attire and my emotions, for Orpha's funeral in three hours. I slid the bike behind a pile of boards.

I stuck my head back inside the front office. "I need to leave my bicycle here for a bit, perhaps until Second . . . I mean, Monday. May I?" I smiled to soften the request.

The woman raised one eyebrow but didn't object. "As you wish. I assume Mr. Sherwood approved your request?"

The Amesbury-bound trolley clanked toward us.

"I'm sure it's not a problem for Jonathan. I thank thee." I shut the door quickly. I was sure, but I didn't want to wait for the Gorgon to go investigate. I dashed across the road and was about to raise my hand to hail the trolley to stop. Instead, a runabout pulled by a handsome dappled gray cut in front of the car.

Luthera herself drove the two-seater open carriage. "Mrs. Dodge, would you like to ride with me?"

The trolley clanged its bell. By pulling over for me, Luthera had blocked its way.

I climbed in. "I thank thee."

The trolley driver clanged the bell again and let out a shout. "Outta my way, lady!"

"We'd better get going," I urged.

Luthera, still in widow's blacks, clucked to the horse. "Let the man stew for a moment. What does it matter if they arrive in town two minutes behind schedule?" She smiled.

This was possibly the first time I'd seen her put on a pleasant face. Up to now she'd been alternately haughty, cold, or dismissive.

"Is Wilson busy today?" I asked.

"I don't know. But there's nothing like driving oneself to get to know a new place, is there?"

"I would have to agree."

"You're not in a hurry, are you?"

I shot her a glance. I did want to speak with Kevin, but spending ladies-only time with Luthera might prove illuminating.

"I need to return home by one o'clock, but it can't be later than eleven right now," I said.

"Good." Her voice turned flat. "Let's make a small excursion."

Uh-oh. This might have been a big error in judgment on my part. She flicked the reins and the horse broke into a trot. I couldn't very well jump out of a moving buggy, not in my condition, not ever.

I cleared my throat. "Did thee hire this horse and carriage?"

"Hire?" She cast me a scornful look. "Mr. Parry kindly lent me them."

Luthera seemed to have an elevated sense of herself and her position in society. It didn't bear speaking of. In my experience, people who regarded themselves as above others often received painful life lessons teaching them otherwise. She would get those lessons in time, or not. It wasn't my place to deliver them.

We drove back toward Main Street without speaking. We passed the stately Union Congregational Church facing the water, crossed the Powow River bridge, then jogged left onto Washington Street to follow the bend in the river. The road was busy with drays and surreys, with shipbuilding shops, the coal depot, and a little farther down, the Merrimac Hat Company with its extensive brick buildings. Luthera was a skilled driver, but she was going too fast for my comfort, coming up close behind slower vehicles and passing them when she could.

The traffic quieted after the bustle of the hat factory, its workers and supplies going in and out. David and I had driven out here two years ago during a full moon, the evening he'd asked me to be his wife.

"Have you deduced yet who killed my husband?" she asked.

I turned my head sharply to look at her. "Why, no. As I said when we first met, investigating a homicide is rightfully the job of the police department."

"You also said you helped them from time to time." She swerved to avoid a hole in the road.

I was glad I'd been holding on tightly. The seat in this carriage rode high, and a passenger could easily be thrown out.

"I know you've been asking questions around town," she continued.

How would she have learned about my inquiries? "I haven't, really." Which was not true, but she didn't need to know that.

Luthera continued. "I'd like to see the scoundrel behind bars before I take my husband's body home."

"I should think thee would."

"I wouldn't be surprised if that Ned Bailey character did it," she said. "He seems a slippery sort."

"Oh?"

"Unctuous. The kind to ingratiate himself with whomever he might garner a favor from."

"But why would he kill Justice?"

She shrugged. "He thought my husband was a competitor, perhaps?"

"Maybe." Although, according to Jonathan, the two had been having a good discussion. On the other hand, Ned was in possession of what was possibly the murder weapon, but I had no intention of revealing what I'd heard. I gazed at an eagle soaring over the river on wide wings, its white head intent on finding fish to catch up in its huge, sharp talons. As intent as Luthera the businesswoman, who didn't seem to be grieving for Justice at all. "Did thee and thy husband have a happy marriage?" I asked.

"What does that have to do with anything?"

"I simply wondered. I was married only in the last year, myself. Thee doesn't seem to be overly sad at his loss."

"Some don't consider it proper to display one's feelings publicly for all to witness." She raised her chin. "I'm not the sniveling little wife, weeping at the drop of a hat."

She certainly was not. "I heard talk about town that thee might be considering a merger with the Parry company."

It was her turn to whip her head over. "Who told you about a merger?"

"Not anyone you would have met."

"Any hearsay about merging is merely gossip." She pressed her lips into a line and focused on the road again. "While I do take an active part in running the business, I'm not at liberty to discuss the plans of Montgomery Carriage Company."

"I only asked because, if thy husband was opposed to the plan, William Parry might have had cause to wish him dead."

"To murder him." She glanced at me again with narrowed eyes. "I wouldn't put it past Mr. Parry. He doesn't seem a completely upright kind of man, if you know what I mean."

The road grew narrower and rougher. My poor full bladder was taking a beating, and I didn't entirely trust Luthera not to do me harm.

"I'm afraid I must be getting home, Luthera, if thee would do me the favor of reversing direction."

When she continued driving, my heart beat faster. What would I do if she attacked me, or tried to throw me from the conveyance?

"Luthera, please turn around." I tried to keep the panic out of my voice.

She didn't speak. My hands chilled, and my throat thickened. Why had I come with her? I should know better by now. The houses out here were spaced far apart, and some of the land at the narrow road's edge was marshy. I had no one to call for help, no way to safely leap out—and then what would I do? She could run me down.

She pulled on the reins and the horse slowed. Now what? I swallowed and gripped the side.

"I'm looking for a wide spot where I have room to turn," she said. "Ah, there's one."

THIRTY-ONE

"WAS I ACTUALLY IN DANGER?" I mused aloud after Luthera dropped me at home — and after I'd recovered from my fright. Or had it been my condition and my imagination leading to my panic out on the river road? In fact, she had not threatened me in the least. And it didn't matter now. I was safe and in my own abode. With the door locked.

After my urgent visit to the water closet, I let down my hair, removed my shoes, and washed up. David had said he'd be home by one o'clock to attend the funeral with me, and it wasn't even noon. I fixed a cold lunch of hard sausage, bread and butter, a boiled egg with prepared mustard, and a couple of dill pickles. I added a glass of cold milk and plopped gratefully into a kitchen chair.

I needed to start more bread rising, as this was our last loaf, but first I would put my feet up and feed myself — and our wee bun in the oven, as Kevin put it, a phrase that made me giggle. It was more like I had a bun in the proofing basket, where a gentle warm temperature led to slow, optimal growth.

Kevin. Had he questioned Ned about the gun? Would Jonathan Sherwood contact Kevin about what he'd seen on the night of the murder? Would Zeb? Questions churned in my brain. I set down my bread and closed my eyes. At this moment, I needed a spot of peace in which to eat and rest. I held Kevin and his team in God's Light. I held Zeb's troubles, too, and the released soul of Justice Harrington. And I held myself and our baby, that peace would return to our town and let me not encounter danger — whether real or imagined — ever again.

I resumed my meal, glancing idly at the newspaper David had left on the table. A story about Alice Sanger caught my eye. In First Month, she became the first woman to be employed in the White House, working for Benjamin Harrison as his presidential secretary. Good for her. Maybe she would blaze the trail for ladies to take other roles in government. I knew my suffragist mother would approve.

Another story announced that intrepid reporter Nellie Bly would be making a New England tour, lecturing about her world travels, with a stop in neighboring Newburyport. I made a note to take Faith. Perhaps John Whittier or someone else could introduce my niece to Nellie.

I turned the page to local news and groaned. Here came the murder right back into my day. A headline screamed, "Carriage Killer Still At Large!" with a subhead of, "Amesbury police lack clues in horrific case." Kevin wasn't going to like this. I certainly didn't.

After popping the last bite of pickle into my mouth, I drained my milk. I should pass along a few bits of information to him, in case he hadn't uncovered them yet. I had no intention of visiting in person, and a telephone call wasn't sufficiently private. But if I wrote a note, I could usually find a boy around on the street who would deliver a missive for payment of a coin, or I could catch the postman on his afternoon rounds.

I moved to the desk in my office, pulling out paper and my cherished Wirt fountain pen. After an initial salutation and an explanation about my recent conversations with several people, I began.

> Zeb Weed says he walked his drunken mother home at about ten that night. The Harringtons were still in the opera house. Zeb thought he heard someone in the alley coughing as if ill with TB. When he returned, he heard someone running. He did not see the body. He also reports W Parry's company has serious financial woes.
>
> Jonathan Sherwood of Lowell's Boat Shop said he saw Ned Bailey, Justice H, and a third man in deep conversation, looking friendly and possibly excited. Check if the third one is a green-eyed Brazilian, possibly named George Amado. Jonathan also witnessed Luthera and Parry discussing a merger of the two companies.
>
> Luthera Harrington offered me a ride home this morning. She said she wants the killer behind bars before she takes her husband's body home, but I expect she has let thee know, as well. She suggested possibly Ned Bailey was the culprit. She would not acknowledge any plans for a merger with Parry and said she doesn't think he is completely upright, whatever that means.

Did I have anything else? I didn't think so. I ended with a few questions.

110

What did Ned say about the gun?
Will thee speak with J Sherwood and Zeb?
Does thee suspect Luthera herself?

I couldn't think of any others.

I am off to Orpha Perkins' funeral at Main Street Congregational this afternoon, followed by a reception at her granddaughter's house on Orchard Street. I would be happy to speak with thee further if thee wishes.

I ended with greetings to his family and my very best wishes. That was all I could do, for now.

THIRTY-TWO

ALMA'S HUSBAND ESCORTED DAVID AND ME to our seats in the Main Street Congregational Church, insisting we sit near the front with Orpha's family. Each tall window was rounded into an arch at the top, with an additional arch over each pair. A simple cross hung at the front. Unlike St. Paul's across the street, where I had attended the funeral of a homicide victim last year, this was not an ornate decor. The sixty-year-old building shared an aspect of light and simplicity with my own beloved Friends Meetinghouse. And differently from St. James, where I'd attended a newborn's funeral mass, the air was not scented with incense, although two fat candles burned in wall sconces at the front.

As the organ played somber music, Faith slid in to sit next to me in the second row. I was glad she'd made it. Orpha had delivered Faith nearly twenty years earlier. Alma, who was seated in front of us next to a couple—likely her parents—twisted in her seat to clasp my hand for a moment. I squeezed and nodded without speaking. Her daughters sat next to their grandmother, the older girl's gaze fixed on the white-covered coffin at the front.

"New dress?" Faith whispered after Alma turned back. "I like it."

I'd changed into my new gray dress. I pointed discreetly to Alma. "She made me two. I am much relieved." I pulled out a handkerchief, expecting I might need it once things got underway. On my other side, David's presence was a solid comfort. After he laid his hand on my knee, I covered it with mine. At a touch on my shoulder from behind, I turned to see Mary Chatigny.

"I'm glad to see thee," I whispered.

She bobbed her head.

A black-robed minister walked down the aisle and climbed the steps to the pulpit to begin the service. I closed my eyes in Quaker prayer, letting the words and responsive readings wash over me. This busyness, this pastor leading the flock, was not my kind of church. I was again grateful I'd been raised as a Friend, a faith in which we each had our own direct connection to God, with no one telling us how to manage it. Each alone decided how to pray, as well as which words to use and when to use them. I knew services like these were a comfort to many. I didn't begrudge them their comfort.

Right now, I wanted only to remember Orpha. All the times she had gently showed me the best technique to help a mother birth her baby. All my visits to her parlor after she gave up the midwifery practice, when she was a wise listener to my feelings and worries. All those peppermints, all those laughs.

I'd been sitting with Orpha's death half the week. But grief welled up in me afresh being here with her as the focus of all present. I began to weep softly and slid off my glasses. I missed her, plain and simple.

The tenor of the service seemed to change. I opened my eyes, wiping them, then restored my spectacles. The minister was finally talking about Orpha. He included a few details about her earlier life I hadn't known.

He looked straight at me. "The family chooses not to speak, but they would be grateful if Mrs. Rose Dodge might share her memories of Mrs. Perkins."

Me? Alma turned in her seat again and gave me an apologetic look, pointing surreptitiously at her father. Why wouldn't he go up and speak about his mother? Or even Alma, although I remembered she'd once told me how terrified she was of public speaking. And she had mentioned what a difficult man her father was.

I rubbed my forehead. I could have prepared some remarks if I'd been forewarned. David patted my knee. Faith whispered that I would do fine. I supposed I would, but I hadn't anticipated having to perform, as it were. I sniffed, took in a deep breath and let it out, then stood. I would let God guide me in my comments, as I did during Friends' worship when I rarely was moved to speak.

"Could you come forward, please, ma'am?" The minister, now down off the pulpit, beckoned.

Faith angled her knees to let me slide past. But when the minister pointed to the pulpit, I shook my head. I faced the mourners at their own level and clasped my hands in front of me, surveying them. In a back pew sat Esther and Akwasi with their newborn bundled in blankets. Orpha had helped them a couple of summers ago. It was early for Esther to be out so soon after the birth. But she'd had an easy time of it. Clearly, they'd both wanted to pay their respects.

"I am midwife Rose Carroll Dodge." I spoke in a loud and clear voice for all to hear. "Many here have known Orpha much longer than I. But when she accepted me as a midwifery apprentice some years ago, she also welcomed me into her life. I have never known anyone as insightful, as caring for the health of mothers and babies, as funny, and as good a listener as Orpha Perkins. That said, she did not suffer fools gladly. Her commentary on the world was acute and right-minded."

Emotion welled up in me once more. Maybe sharing my memories and feelings about my favorite octogenarian was going to be more difficult than I'd expected. I swallowed hard and gazed across the pews. Jeanette and Frannie were there, with Annie next to them. I spied Jonathan and Amy Sherwood, the latter wiping her eyes. Catherine Toomey sat in front of them, also patting the corners of her eyes with a handkerchief. Even John Whittier was there. He'd been acquainted with Orpha, and I was glad to see him well enough to be out.

My survey stopped short at William Parry toward the back. What was he doing here? Perhaps Orpha had delivered his first son, the one who had ended up murdered, and William had come to pay his respects.

At least Kevin was not in evidence today. He had lurked in the back at other funerals and memorials I'd attended. This one didn't have anything to do with a homicide, for which I was grateful.

More words came to me. "Orpha could see into one's true soul. I am grateful for the years I had with her and for her teaching. I'm most grateful for her friendship, and I know each of thee here will miss her as much as I will. Remember, she would not want thee to walk about with a heavy step because of her absence. Orpha loved life and celebrated it, as we celebrate her. May her soul rest easily in God's arms." I closed my eyes and prayed for her. Even as I did, my wee bun stirred again, as if also in homage to Orpha.

The minister cleared his throat and murmured a soft *thank you*, which roused me. I resumed my seat. He ended the service with the hymn "Amazing Grace." It was rousing and simple, and I knew Orpha loved it. Alma must have requested the song be included.

"All present are invited to join for fellowship at Mr. and Mrs. Latting's home." The minister gave Alma's Orchard Street address. "Burial in the Mount Prospect Cemetery will take place at a later date after the ground thaws." The organ started up again with another somber tune barely short of a dirge. The minister gestured to Alma and her family, including her parents, to walk out with him, no doubt to greet mourners on the broad front steps of the church.

THIRTY-THREE

FAITH WHISPERED, "I want to get home to Zeb. I'll see thee tomorrow in worship."

I gave her a quick hug. Even though it took a few minutes before David and I made it outside, small groups of people lingered. Some stood on the wide landing under a portico supported by four two-story-high columns. Others conversed on the equally wide steps. The family reception line had broken up, but the minister remained. David and I greeted him.

"You looked surprised in there to be invited to share your memories," the minister said to me. "I apologize for putting you on the spot. I thought the family would have asked you before the service began."

"It was fine. I'm not a timid person, and I owe Orpha an enormous debt." I spied William coughing into his handkerchief. Mary Chatigny gazed at him, too, with a worried expression. "If thee will excuse me."

"I'll wait here," David said. "Reverend, what can you tell me about this venerable building?"

William started on the long walkway to the street, which ran down the middle of a grassy lawn.

"William," I called.

He whirled, wearing a scowl.

I grew near but stopped about six feet away. If he had tuberculosis, getting any closer could imperil my health and my baby's.

"I was surprised to see thee at the service," I began. "Did thee know Orpha?"

"Yes." His scowl slipped away. "In my opinion, she was one of the truly good people in this world."

"Did she deliver Thomas?"

"She did, and she helped my late first wife through a difficult labor. I was extraordinarily grateful for Mrs. Perkins."

I had delivered his second and third children—from different mothers—in the space of a month two years ago. Those mothers had not had such happy outcomes, and I doubted he was grateful to me.

116

"I heard something of interest this morning," I began. "Is it true thee plans to merge thy business concern with the Montgomery company of Ottawa, Canada?"

Alarm flew into his eyes for a brief moment. He blinked and shifted his gaze away from my face. "Where could you have heard such a ridiculous thing?"

I waited without answering.

"That's complete nonsense," he blustered, folding his arms on his chest. "I have no plans in the least to undertake such a business maneuver. Whoever told you is full of hogwash. Good day, Mrs. Dodge." He touched his bowler and strode down the path.

Well. Doth someone protest too much?

"Rose," a woman's voice called from in front of the church. Frannie waved at me from where she stood with Catherine, Jeanette, Annie, and Mary.

I joined them. "Mary, does thee know my friends, and my partner, Annie?"

She smiled. "They've introduced themselves."

"We've lost a jewel," Catherine said. "Mrs. Perkins delivered my Patrick yon these thirty years."

"And my daughter, too," Frannie offered.

"My children, as well," Mary said. She gazed at the street, where William had already turned onto the sidewalk. "And a child of his, I suppose."

"Yes, his first," I said. "William doesn't seem at all well."

"He's not." Mary pressed her lips together. "And he should be resting at home, not gallivanting around to funerals."

"Rose, have you untangled the matter of the murder yet?" Annie asked me.

"Not exactly." I surveyed the group's eager expressions. All but Mary knew me well, and they were acquainted with my history assisting on official investigations. "I did report to the police what thy maid saw, Frannie, and the new acting chief — that is, Kevin — is looking into it. But I'm afraid the facts of the case are still quite murky. Does any of thee know Ned Bailey personally?"

"Not I," Mary said.

Catherine and Frannie shook their heads.

"He's my husband's cousin's wife's nephew," Jeanette offered.

"That's a convoluted connection," I said.

She laughed and slapped her thigh. "Isn't it? Still, Mr. Papka's family loves big gatherings. I've sat with Ned a few times at summer picnics and whatnot."

"He mentioned to me he was excited about a plan for a horseless motorcar," I said in a quiet voice. "And he was seen in intense conversation with Justice Harrington the night of the murder. Does thee think, Jeanette, thee could ask thy husband to inquire of his cousin's wife about any business dealings between the two?"

Jeanette shook her head. "I would, but the cousin and his wife were called away to Vermont to her mother's deathbed."

Drat the luck. "And thee doesn't know of any dealings?" I asked her.

"No, but I'll see what I can learn."

"Thank thee."

"What about the wife?" Catherine asked. "I told you how she was being scornful and insulting to her husband before he was killed."

"You did," I said. "I believe Kevin regards her with interest in terms of being a possible culprit."

"But not your nephew-in-law, I hope," Jeanette said.

"Good heavens, no," I said. "Zeb is innocent of any wrongdoing, and I think I have convinced Kevin of such."

Mary followed our volleying of questions and answers with an amused expression.

"His mother's quite the tippler, isn't she?" Catherine murmured.

"I've heard the same." Frannie snorted. "We all have our weaknesses, though, don't we? I, for one, can't resist a good pipe of tobacco."

I stared at her. Frannie smoked a pipe? I had no idea.

"Give me chocolate any day," Jeanette added. "In any form."

Catherine nodded. "For me it's ale. There's nothing like a cold tankard to relax a soul."

I supposed my weakness was wanting to tease out the facts of a mystery, which was not my job in the least.

Mary gave a little enigmatic smile. "I have no minor vices."

I blinked, trying to sort out what she meant. Did she have a major vice?

David waved at me from the church. I held up a finger, signaling I'd be along in a minute. "Who else is going to Alma's?"

THIRTY-FOUR

ALMA'S HOUSE WAS PACKED WITH MOURNERS, and the dining table groaned with the food the ladies had prepared. I tasted a savory lamb tart, a chicken dumpling, and a miniature deep-fried fishcake. Perhaps this could take the place of our supper at home. Sweet treats also abounded, as did tea, sherry, and some other spirit. David helped himself to a plate, as well as a small glass of what looked like whiskey.

Alma's mother particularly thanked me for helping care for Orpha and for my message during the funeral. "You took my place at her deathbed, and I will be ever indebted." She glanced at her cantankerous husband and lowered her voice. "I simply couldn't get away."

Alma's father, on the other hand, was perfunctory in his greeting to the point of curtness. Alma's little girls, now five and seven, were helpful for a bit, offering to take visitors' coats and directing them to the food, but they eventually disappeared to play.

I still found it painful to be in the house where my mentor had lived the entire time I'd known her. I could see David was eager to leave. He'd had a long conversation with Mary about things medical, then had ended up in polite congress with Alma's husband. When I suggested we depart, his relief was tangible.

The sun was sinking below the trees as David and I strolled toward home, my hand comfortably tucked through his arm. Today had augured spring more than recent ones, with a moderate temperature and only a slight breeze.

"I would have thought the ground would be soft enough by now for a burial," I said.

"Perhaps it is. What he said could have been an excuse to hold a private burial tomorrow or one day soon."

"So a Congregational minister would lie for the convenience of the family?" I glanced up at him.

"Maybe." He laughed softly. "He's quite the interesting man. We had ourselves an architectural conversation while you ladies were plotting who knows what. Did you know the church building was constructed for the Unitarian Congregational Society in 1829 and was acquired by the current denomination only three years later?"

"I didn't." We'd turned from Greenleaf onto Whittier Street when a high-stepping gelding pulling a Stanhope gig at a fast clip passed us. Had I seen Ned Bailey driving it?

David pulled me closer but winced at the sudden movement.

"What's wrong, my love?" I asked him.

"It's one of my headaches."

I stroked his arm. "We'll be home in a minute. Thee has kept me company all afternoon, and I'm grateful. But thee works hard and needs to rest more."

The driver pulled to a halt ahead of us. Ned Bailey leaned out. "What ho, Dodges!" He held the reins as he doffed his hat. "I was on my way to have a word with Mrs. Dodge. You know, with her investigative prowess and such." His voice shook slightly. From exertion or with nerves?

David and I exchanged a glance. He raised his eyebrows at me. I shrugged.

"We're only yards from home," I said to Ned. "Please meet us there."

Ned drove on, crossing Sparhawk and pulling up in front of our lovely home. He climbed down, keeping the reins in his hand.

"I'll speak with him outside," I murmured to David as we walked. "Thee should go in and lie down."

"I shall." He squeezed my hand.

When we arrived and David had gone into the house, I said to Ned, "What can I help thee with? I have only a few minutes." I wanted to go inside to minister to my husband, to make sure he was comfortable and had a cold compress at hand.

"Well, then. You see." He cleared his throat. "Your detective seems to be rather interested in, ah, the matter of my motorcar ideas. You remember what I mentioned to you at the Board of Trade meeting?"

I nodded and waited for more. I expected — or rather, hoped — Kevin was also interested in the matter of the weapon. But would Ned mention the pistol?

"I had given my proposal to Mr. Justice Harrington," he continued. "He was quite excited to work together on such a forward-thinking idea."

"Thee gave him the plans for the motorcar?"

"Yes. But only as a loan, you see. So he could get a sense of the scope. He was to return them the next day."

"Thee must have made a copy first."

"Alas, I did not. Now Donovan seems to think Harrington absconded with the plans against my will. He hinted I shot the Canadian for his troubles."

I eyed him. "Did thee?"

"Mrs. Dodge!" He gave his head a quick shake. "No. I did not."

If Ned had killed Justice, he wouldn't tell me, anyway.

"Were the plans recovered?" I asked.

He gave me a baleful look. "They were not, more's the pity."

"I wonder what happened to the papers," I mused, more to myself than to him. Kevin could be right. Ned could be dissembling about all this to hide the fact he shot Justice and took his plans back. Or, if someone else was the killer, that person could have simply tossed them into the rushing Powow River, and they would never been seen again. I again wondered why the murderer had left the weapon and not thrown it in the river.

"Ned, I hear thee kept the gun for safekeeping. The murder weapon."

"Gun?" Tiny pearls of sweat broke out on his forehead. "Where did you . . . I mean, I don't know about a gun."

"If thee has a gun thee found the night of the murder, thee needs to tell the police." Except surely Kevin had asked him about it. And possibly searched the house and confiscated the weapon. "Thee must do the right thing."

He lifted his chin. "I'm getting along to the evening event, if that's what you mean." An odd expression came over his face.

Dark was falling. For all I knew, Ned had shot Justice himself. And he was acting strangely. I'd better get myself inside, and fast.

"I wish thee luck rewriting thy ideas, Ned. I must take my leave and let thee get along to thy event." I smiled.

"Wait." He clasped my forearm. "You have to help me!"

With what? "Excuse me." I pulled up to my full height and stared at his hand until he dropped it. "It's not my job to find a murderer nor to assist thee. I wish thee luck sorting out the facts."

He scowled at me but finally climbed back into the carriage, muttering to himself.

I waited, hands clasped in front of me, until he clucked to the horse and drove off. Ned had always seemed something of a buffoon, and I'd never felt threatened by him before. Right now the lamplight spilling from the front window of my home extended its comfort in the most reassuring of ways.

THIRTY-FIVE

AFTER DAVID AND I SUPPED ON A BOWL OF SOUP an hour later, he said he was going to bed. I sat in the lamplight letting out the side seams of an older dress of mine. I'd remembered the seamstress telling me she always made fat double seams in dresses for ladies of my age, expecting a pregnancy to come along before the dress had outlived its purpose. I wanted something comfortable to wear while cooking and doing chores so my new garments didn't get stained. This dress would be perfect for that. I made a note to check the dark rose-colored dress Alma had made last fall for my marriage. It might have the same feature.

I was worried about David's headaches. I prayed they didn't signal a deeper health problem. What if he had some kind of tumor on the brain? He was a medical doctor, but he still might be ignoring the severity or significance of his pains. I loved him deeply and didn't want him to suffer so. Also, our future as a happy family would be at risk if he were stricken. I resolved I would urge him to seek treatment, to find a specialist without delay.

When the telephone rang, I hurried to answer it before it awoke David. It was Kevin on the line, asking if he might come over to talk through the case. I glanced at the clock. It was only seven o'clock.

"Please do," I told him. "I have a bit of new information."

"Excellent. I'll be along within the half hour. Thank you, Miss Rose."

He arrived fifteen minutes later. After I cautioned him to keep his voice down so we didn't wake David upstairs, we sat in the sitting room. I picked up my sewing project while he pulled out a slip of paper. I recognized it as my letter to him from this morning.

"I thank you for this missive, Miss Rose." He chuckled. "I suppose I should have been calling you Mrs. Rose for the last six months, but I'm not a young man and am afraid I'm rather set in my ways."

"Thee is not a spring chicken, but thee is not old, Kevin. Anyway, I don't have a problem with thee using Miss Rose."

He tapped a finger on the letter. "You asked me a few questions here. I'll see if I'm able to address them, and then perhaps we can discuss a few other matters."

"Very well."

"I have heard about the Parry outfit being mismanaged. I haven't been able to track down Ned Bailey today, nor Mr. Sherwood."

"But did thee talk with Ned yesterday about the gun?"

He made an exasperated sound. "The man says he merely found it and didn't want anyone to be hurt."

"So he secreted it in his underthings? Hiding a weapon not his own doesn't make sense."

Kevin's cheeks reddened at hearing the location of the gun. "No, it does not. He rightly should have found the nearest patrolman and turned it in."

"Was it the size of the gun Justice was shot with?"

"As you're aware, we have no way of knowing exactly, but it appears it could have been, from the caliber of the weapon and the size of Harrington's wounds."

"Thee no longer is interested in Zeb Weed, I hope."

"Haven't ruled him out completely, but he's farther down my list at this point." Kevin peered at the letter. "This business of hearing coughing, now."

"William Parry has tuberculosis. His doctor has confirmed it."

"Oh? What's his name, this doctor?"

"Mary Chatigny." I stifled a snort as I watched his jaw drop at hearing her first name. "Her consulting office is on the corner of Elm and Marston."

"You ladies are making quite the strides, aren't you? What will be next? The vote?"

"I certainly hope so." I smiled. "But about William Parry, I spoke with him after Orpha's funeral. He protested rather too strongly that he has no plans to merge with the Montgomery enterprise. I think a possible business deal bears looking into further."

"Duly noted." In fact, he drew a pencil out of his pocket and scribbled on the paper.

"Now, what about Luthera?" I asked. "Has thee had additional conversations with her?"

"The wife. Who seems to regard herself rather highly."

"She does."

"I attempted to engage her in a round of questions this very afternoon. She was not receptive to the idea, saying she had important business to conduct." He raised his eyebrows and tossed his head when he said "business."

"But you're the police. The chief of police."

"You'd think that might have held some sway, but no. She claimed a kind of exemption because she's from Canada." He clapped his hands on the tops of his legs. "This is a thorny case, Miss Rose, and it's more frustrating than a bachelor with . . ." He let his voice trail off as his face reddened anew. "It's frustrating. I'll leave it at that."

Which was a blessing. Kevin Donovan was a man of his times. I suspected his language was much saltier when he was in the company of his male colleagues. I picked out another few stitches.

"Ned Bailey stopped by here at dusk," I said. "He told me he wanted my help, or some such thing."

"Did he now?"

I nodded. "He said he had lent Justice Harrington his plans for his new motorcar. He said Justice was excited about them. And now the plans have disappeared, and Ned hadn't made a copy. No one found any papers with the body?"

"No." Kevin stretched out the word. "If Parry killed Harrington, he could have absconded with the plans thinking it would help rescue his company."

"That would be a tenuous plan, at best. Surely it would require capital to make such a vehicle, not to mention much wooing of customers to win them over to the idea of a carriage driving under its own power."

"Yes, but Parry might be feeling desperate about his prospects."

"Or Luthera could have been angry Justice was taking the company on a path she didn't approve of," I mused. "She might have killed her husband and tossed the plans in the river."

"Do you think Bailey was dissembling with the entire story, trying to hide what he'd done?"

"I wondered the same, but I truly don't know."

"Perhaps we're both on the wrong track," Kevin said. "It could have been the work of some lunatic unrelated to any of this carriage business."

I tilted my head. "How often do crazy people commit murder?"

Kevin grunted. "Not very often. We fortunately have a low population of lunatics in Amesbury at present. Perhaps our culprit is another one of these foreigners swarming our town this week. You can't trust them, you know. All manner of swarthy types are about. Greeks and Brazilians, even two Arabs from Egypt, of all places. And I spied a gent with skin as black as night. Well dressed and comported, to be sure."

"Kevin, watch thy prejudices. Simply because the visitors don't look like thee doesn't mean they are criminals."

"I know. You're always schooling me about my judgments. You yourself mentioned this Amado character was talking with Harrington and Bailey, though. He could have done in Harrington and made off with the plans."

"He could have, and maybe he did, but not because he hails from Brazil."

The tall case clock in the front hall chimed eight soft tones.

Kevin jumped up. "My sainted Emmaline is waiting supper at home for me. And I'm late."

I started to stand, mending and all.

"Don't yeh be after thinking of getting up, Miss Rose." His Irish brogue always increased when he was feeling pressure or was in a hurry. "I'll be lettin' myself out."

"Good night, Kevin," I called after him. He was a smart man and a good detective. But why wasn't a killer behind bars instead of somewhere on Amesbury's streets? And, because at large was exactly where the murderer was, I did get up after the door closed. I clicked the lock firmly shut and drew tight against the night the last two open curtains.

THIRTY-SIX

A LIGHT RAIN FELL as I walked the ten minutes to the Friends Meetinghouse the next morning wearing my oiled cloak. David had offered to drive me in the buggy, but I'd said I wanted the time to clear my head. His headache was blessedly gone, but he'd chosen to stay quietly at home and catch up on his medical journals. He'd also hinted he might be concocting a delicious midday meal for us, which had gained him an extra kiss. I decided to postpone my conversation with him about seeking a headache consultation until later today.

I hung my cloak on a peg in the front hall and slid into a pew at a few minutes before ten. Faith and Zeb hurried in and sat next to me. I folded my hands and closed my eyes, ready to let the outer world slip away and leave God alone, as John Whittier had written in his poem about this very Meetinghouse. I held Kevin in the Light for solving the case. I held my dear David, that his headaches might cease recurring. And I held in God's Light our growing child, who, now that I was quiet, made tiny flips within me.

After the rustling of latecomers stilled, I opened my eyes and glanced around. On the opposite side of the room was Prudence next to her husband. Sober, I hoped. John sat erect on the facing bench with the other elders, as he always did. My eyes flew wide open when my gaze fell on a pew near where John sat. The man I saw was Amado, the Brazilian, and he was staring straight at me. I closed my eyes, not acknowledging him. Was he a Friend? Were there Quakers in Brazil? Or . . . did he even live in Brazil? Perhaps he'd immigrated to our commonwealth and lived in a nearby city or even in Boston.

I'd only once been more surprised by someone's presence at worship. It had been when a disturbed man had tried to set the Meetinghouse on fire two years ago. For now, I attempted to slow my breathing. I wouldn't find the peace I sought—nay, desperately needed—by letting my brain dwell on unanswered questions.

And thus the worship passed in silence. This week no one was moved to stand and share a message from God, for which I was grateful. I always felt blessedly restored from a full hour of silence. As the church bells in town started to toll eleven, an elder stood and began the handshake of fellowship. After some moments of greetings, I filed out with Faith and Zeb.

"Zeb," I murmured. "Did thee see the Brazilian thee mentioned? Amado?"

"I did. I don't know what he's doing here."

"Neither do I." But I waited to the side of the front steps. The rain had dwindled to a mist.

When nearly everyone had emerged, John walked out on the arm of the dashing Amado.

"Ah, Rose dear," John said. "Has thee met our visitor?"

"Not to speak with. I am Rose Dodge." I extended my gloved hand.

Instead of shaking it, the Brazilian lifted it toward his face. I opened my mouth to object, but it was too late. He pressed my hand to his lips, then relinquished it.

"*Mrs.* Rose Dodge." I stressed my title, something I usually avoided. I wanted to be sure this flirtatious man knew I was married.

"I am Jorge Amado." He pronounced his Christian name *Zhor-zhee*, as Zeb had. "I am honored to make the acquaintance of this famous man's friend." He gave a little bow, but as he straightened, he winked at me. He spoke with quite a strong accent, as Zeb had mentioned, but his words were perfect English. "I have sought out the great poet because I, too, dabble in the art."

"He's written some very nice pieces," John said. "Alas, I can only read them in translation."

"And I am very curious about your faith." Jorge gestured to the Meetinghouse behind him. "I have never met a Quaker in my native Rio de Janeiro."

"Thee is welcome to worship with us at any time," I said. "And John is indeed a great poet." I smiled at my elderly friend. Looking back at Jorge, I said, "How is thee finding our fair city? It's quite different from Brazil, I should imagine."

He laughed heartily. "Yes it is, in many ways. The food, the sea, the ladies, and of course, the weather. But alas, I now live in Boston."

"And thee works in the carriage industry?" I asked.

"I have a position of some responsibility in the design department of the Kimball Brothers Carriage Company."

An esteemed Boston producer of carriages. Which could make him very interested in Ned's plans.

John inclined his head. "We are sorry thee had to be here during a week when one of thy peers was murdered."

"Yes," Jorge said. "It was shocking to hear of Mr. Harrington's death. I had quite an interesting conversation with him the evening of the banquet. In fact, it was only a few hours after I first set my gaze on this lovely lady in front of us."

I ignored the flash of his smile. "I understand thee discussed Ned Bailey's revolutionary new plans."

John shifted his gaze to me, looking surprised.

Jorge's slick demeanor wobbled for a split second. He gazed over my shoulder. "Yes, and it was a remarkable idea. I understand the plans have sadly been lost."

"Did Ned tell thee so?" I asked.

"No." He brought the green focus back to my face. "It was someone else in the town. I can't recall at this moment."

I watched him. I smelled a lie, but I wasn't sure if it was about the plans or about who told him they were gone. As far as I knew, the loss of the papers had not been in the news.

John cleared his throat. "This kind gentleman has agreed to walk me home. *Vamos*, Jorge?" A little smile played at John's lips. "I convinced him to teach me a few words of Portuguese," he whispered loudly to me.

"*Vamos*. A pleasure to speak with you, Mrs. Dodge." He also stressed the *Mrs.*, his manner again as smooth as new cream.

"And I thee" I said.

They made their way slowly down the walk and turned onto Friend Street. Rather than answering my questions, this encounter had only added to them. Oh, well. I was accustomed to inquiries leading to more questions. I took a step toward the gate onto Greenleaf Street and my own route homeward.

"Rose," a woman called out from behind me.

I turned to see Prudence with her hand raised. Where had she been hiding? I waited until she reached me.

"Hello, Prudence." I peered at her face, but she didn't seem to be under the influence of spirits at this moment. *Good.*

"I understand I missed Orpha's funeral," she began. "I am exceedingly sorry."

"Yes, it was yesterday. And a lovely service, too."

"I was, ah, indisposed."

I could guess at how. "I didn't realize thee knew her."

"Certainly I did. She delivered my babies, and I taught her granddaughter music. Back when I was teaching."

Of course Alma had mentioned that. And the reason Prudence had stopped teaching, too.

"Is Alma . . . doing well?" she asked.

"Very well, yes, and she did an admirable job caring for Orpha in the end. Alma has a successful business as a dressmaker, too."

"I'm glad." She stared at her clasped hands, then up into my face. "Zebulon tells me thee is looking into the awful killing."

"I only assist the police with ideas. They are investigating, not I."

"But suppose . . ." Her voice trailed off.

Once again I waited. Not patiently this time. I wanted to get home and avail myself of the water closet.

"What if someone saw something but didn't want to go to the authorities with the information?"

Someone. *Like her?* "That would be the right thing to do. The police don't bite."

She wrinkled her nose. "No, but they are rather too well acquainted with . . . with this person."

"This person could tell me. Or this person could possibly write an anonymous note and have it delivered to the proper person."

She nodded slowly as if neither of those options were acceptable.

I touched her arm. "Prudence, is this person thee?" I kept my voice gentle. "Thee must tell me what thee saw."

She let out a shuddering breath and glanced around. We were the only two left in front of the forty-year-old building. The mist turned back to rain and began to patter on my hood.

"It's this way. I slipped out again after Zeb took me home that night. I'm an ill woman, Rose. I seek out my poison even when I know I should not. The tavern keeper slips me a pint out the back door from time to time."

She must be ill, if she was wandering the streets alone late at night in search of more alcohol. I was surprised she was still alive.

"And," she continued, "I saw the poor man's dead body. Someone was pilfering it."

"What does thee mean?"

Her eyes wide, she said, "A man removed a sheaf of papers from the corpse's coat."

The plans. "Did thee see who it was?"

"I did," she whispered. "It was that gentleman who sat near Friend John during worship."

THIRTY-SEVEN

DAVID AND I SAT IN OUR DINING ROOM at one o'clock, holding hands across the corner of the table in a moment of silent grace. I did my best to quash thoughts of Prudence's shocking piece of information, although that was all I'd been able to think of as I'd strolled home.

I now opened my eyes, squeezed his hand, and surveyed the feast on the table. He'd roasted a fat chicken and added potatoes and rosemary to the pan in the last hour. The aromatic potatoes glistened with the roasting fats on the serving platter next to the carved chicken. A dish of stewed squash and apples sat next to it, with a cold salad of sliced beets sprinkled with fresh parsley on the side.

I'd been nurturing several pots of fresh herbs all winter in a sunny kitchen window. At this time of year, green food to eat was in short supply at the market, or fresh anything, truly. Today's beets, apples, squash, and potatoes had all come out of the root cellar.

We talked about all and sundry as we ate.

"This morning I read about a new medical device being developed, Rose," David said. "It's designed to used electrical signals to amplify weak sounds into stronger ones."

"For the deaf and hard of hearing?"

"Yes," he said. "It's quite promising, although not quite at the point of being manufactured."

"It will be soon, I have no doubt. And I met my first Brazilian."

"Here for the Spring Opening?"

"Yes. His name is Jorge Amado, and he accompanied John Whittier to Meeting for Worship."

"It's remarkable someone would come all the way from the Southern Hemisphere to buy carriages."

I swallowed a bite of tender, juicy chicken. "He said he lives in Boston now. It wasn't quite as long a trip. Some visitors here this week are from as far away as Australia, truly the other side of the world." I stared at my plate, frowning, thinking about Jorge absconding with Ned's plans.

David reached out to cover my hand. "What is it, dear Rose?"

"Nothing I should bother thee with."

"Dear wife, there is nothing you should *not* bother me with. And I sense it is not the excellence of the meal you frown about."

I met his gaze. "This is a delicious, beautiful, superlative dinner, dear husband, and I thank thee. And thee knows me too well. This Jorge said something about the night of the murder which is picking at my brain."

"Your picking is my picking. Please share if you feel so inclined. It might help to talk it all through." He patted my hand and returned to his chicken.

"I feel as if a puzzle piece has fallen into place, and I appreciate thy offer. But I truly don't want to sully our meal together with talk of homicide. I'll try to find Kevin later, or at least write him a note, to share my thoughts." I smiled, hoping I had not hurt David's feelings.

When he gave me an understanding nod, I counted my blessings in husband yet once again.

"I heard that a new musical performance is coming to the opera house next month," I said brightly. "Perhaps we can obtain tickets and have a night out."

"While you still can. I like your idea, Rose. Did I ever tell you about the time I saw *The Mikado* in Portsmouth?"

And so we passed the rest of the meal. But by two o'clock, thoughts of last week's crime again filled my brain. It was First Day, the day of rest. I should be sitting with my husband in quiet companionship, knitting and reading, chatting and writing. Instead, after I cleaned up the kitchen, I put through a call to the police station.

"The chief is at home, Mrs. Dodge," the officer told me. "It's Sunday, you know."

"I do know. I thank thee." I hung the receiver on its hook, considering my options. I rather urgently wanted Kevin to know how Jorge had reacted to my questions and what Prudence had said about seeing him steal the papers from Justice Harrington's dead body. Perhaps the Brazilian had killed the Canadian to obtain the innovative plans. If they'd tussled in the alley, Jorge could have pulled out a pistol and shot him in the heat of the moment. South Americans were supposed to be passionate, weren't they?

Either way, I had to tell Kevin. Should I place a call to him at home? Write a letter? Pay him a visit? I knew Emmaline would welcome me.

But I shouldn't disturb his day of rest with his family. And it could all wait until tomorrow. Couldn't it?

I gazed out the front window. The rain beat in from the west, wind tapping it on the glass. Behind me David snored lightly in his chair. I again prayed his headaches weren't the sign of some other malady. They plagued him with some regularity, and the next day he was always exhausted.

The facts of this murder were currently plaguing me. They weren't exhausting so much as frustrating. The rain made me disinclined to go out again, whether alone or with David. This news was far too important to risk Gertrude listening in to a telephone call. Pen and paper would again have to suffice.

I sat at the desk in my office and began to write. I could solve the problem of how to get my letter to the detective when I was done. I'd penned only the opening salutation when a sharp rap came at the side door.

"Faith," I exclaimed at the sight of her under a huge black umbrella now dripping rain on the covered veranda. "Come in."

She left the umbrella outside and hurried inside. "Rose, you wouldn't believe what I just learned." She flipped back her bonnet and swiped rain off her forehead. Her eyes were wide, and her hair was escaping its pins.

"Please tell me." Was this about the Spring Opening murder?

"Well, I went into the *Daily News* office, even though it's First Day. I needed to hand in my story about last night's Board of Trade gala."

"Was it the final gathering of the week?" I asked.

"No. There's one more closing ceremony at the end of the day today. Too bad about the rain." She wrinkled her nose. "The ceremony was to have been outside with a parade of carriages."

"That is a pity." I waited, but Faith only gazed out the window. I cleared my throat. "I'm sorry I interrupted thee, Faith. Please go on."

She started, then laughed. "I almost forgot I came here with news. So, I went into the office, and the man who covers the police was furiously typing. We were the only two in there. I asked him what had happened. Rose, thee won't believe it."

Instead of strangling her, I raised my eyebrows. "Tell me."

"They've brought in that handsome Brazilian under suspicion of committing homicide! The case is solved, Rose."

Maybe. "Jorge Amado." I narrowed my eyes. "Did this police reporter say what the evidence was?"

"A witness saw him with the victim's body in the alley the night of the murder."

"Who was the witness?"

"He didn't have a name," Faith said. "But I knew you would want to know right away."

I folded my arms, thinking. Either Prudence had overcome her worries about going to the police or someone else had seen Jorge with dead Justice.

"I thank thee for telling me. But this witness didn't see the killing, correct?"

"I don't think so."

"Ah. And was Kevin's name bandied about?"

She shook her head. "The reporter didn't mention it."

Kevin might not even know about it. Unless his day of rest had been rudely interrupted by someone else.

"Did anything of interest happen last night?" I asked. "Wait. I should clarify my question. Did thee overhear any interactions with Luthera Harrington, Ned Bailey, or William Parry that sparked thy interest? Or which might have sparked mine?" Kevin's interest, to put it more accurately.

She blinked. "Hmm. Let me think."

The telephone jangled and I grabbed for it before it awoke David.

"Miss Rose, this is Kevin. Can you come down to the station? We might have a development."

"I certainly can. I will see thee shortly." I hung up the receiver as David padded in on stocking feet, still looking sleepy. So much for not awakening him.

"Who will you see shortly?" he asked. "Oh, hello, Faith."

She smiled at him.

"Kevin wants to see me at the station," I said. "He might have had a breakthrough." But did he have the right person in custody?

"I'll drive you." David instantly looked more alert. Responding to a sudden request for services was a skill doctors had in equal measure with midwives.

"David." Faith held up her hand. "I have a hansom cab waiting. Rose can go into town with me."

"Yes, let me do that." I stood. "Thee must keep relaxing, my dear."

"Call me if you want me to bring you home," David said. "It's raining buckets out there."

He smoothed my hair, a gesture that made me want to stay home and possibly take him directly upstairs to our bed. Pregnancy hadn't diminished my carnal desires in the slightest. If anything, they'd increased. But duty called.

"Give me two minutes to get ready," I told Faith. I kissed David's cheek and pointed myself toward the all-important water closet. The last thing I wanted was to be in need of facilities while I was in the police station. One could only imagine the hygienic state of whatever an all-male department used for their needs.

THIRTY-EIGHT

FAITH AND I BUMPED ALONG IN THE BACKSEAT OF THE HANSOM, a carriage that had seen better days. The side flaps were down but rain still found its way in. We huddled together in the middle, trying to avoid getting even wetter.

"Rose, thee asked about seeing Ned Bailey last night," Faith said softly, even though the driver was outside our compartment. "He was there, and he seemed to be avoiding Luthera Harrington. He seemed, I don't know, uncomfortable."

Interesting. The night of the murder, he'd apparently been in intense conversation with her husband.

"Was Luthera responding in kind?"

"She kept casting him glances. I saw her go over to engage him in conversation once, but he turned his back and stepped away. It was blatantly rude of him."

"It is. He usually comes across as eager to please." I thought. "What about William Parry?"

"Him." She tossed her head. "He was the eager one. He was fluttering about near Luthera. But once he began coughing. she nearly pushed him away."

"I don't blame her. He shouldn't even be out."

The driver pulled up to the police station.

"Is thee off to home, Faith?" I asked.

"No, I'm going to the closing ceremony. They're holding it indoors at the opera house."

"I thank thee for the transport." I kissed her cheek, pulled up my hood, and climbed down. A couple of minutes later I faced Kevin across his desk, having exchanged greetings. "Do share the development of which thee spoke."

He sat back and folded his arms, wearing a satisfied smile. "Thanks to you, I expect, Mrs. Weed the elder came in and told us she'd witnessed Mr. George Amado take papers off the corpse. He's in a cell in the back right now."

"Good. Was Prudence sober?"

"Yes. By some miracle, she was."

"What does Jorge say about the papers?" I asked.

He gaped. *"Zhor-zhee?* What now, Miss Rose?"

"That's how his name is properly said. It's the Portuguese version of George."

Kevin rolled his eyes.

"Anyway, were the papers Ned's plans?" I asked.

"The man has shut his mouth tighter than a vise. Claims he needs to speak to the Brazilian consulate," Kevin growled. "We have entirely too many uncooperative foreigners around here this week."

I didn't envy him his job. "Prudence told me she didn't witness the murder, only the theft. Does thee think Jorge killed Justice?"

The satisfied look slid off the detective's face. "I'd like to think so, but the fact of the matter is, I have no evidence to that effect."

"Nor an eyewitness," I pointed out.

"Not that, either. Confound it, Miss Rose." He pulled his light brows together.

"What about William Parry? Has thee had additional talks with him?"

"No. But I did receive an interesting communication from the senior Bailey household. Mrs. Bailey wished me to know her husband is unfortunately as mad as a March hare."

"He suffers from the dementia of old age," I said. The poor man. What a blessing my dear Orpha had not been afflicted with that kind of decline in mental acuity.

"Yes. He apparently never had plans for a new design. My mother would have said he's gone completely seafóid." Kevin pointed to his head. "You know, he's not the full shilling."

I smiled at the image. "And therefore his plans weren't stolen," I mused. "That clears up one question, at least."

"Yes. He imagined the whole thing."

"Sir?" A young patrolman popped his head into the doorway. "A Mr. Ned Bailey is here asking to speak with you. He says it concerns the homicide."

Kevin's eyebrows ascended nearly to his hairline. "Show him in forthwith, by all means."

"This could prove important," I said. "Does thee want me to absent myself?"

"Not at all," he scoffed. "You stay right there, Miss Rose."

After Ned was ushered in, Kevin barked at the young officer to fetch another chair. Ned perched on the edge of it, kneading his bowler in his hands. And not speaking.

"Well, Mr. Bailey? What do you have to tell us?" Kevin asked.

Ned stared at his hat, rolling its edge in his fingers so hard I thought a piece of the rim might detach. He gazed up at me instead of at his questioner.

"It's like this. Yesterday Mrs. Dodge counseled me to do the right thing. And I went to church this morning at St. James and prayed." He swallowed. Again the pearls of sweat dotted his brow. "I have a confession I would like to make."

A confession of murder? This could be exactly what we needed, although I would be surprised if Ned had intentional homicide in him. An accident resulting in death was more likely. I waited.

Kevin drummed his fingers on the desk. He shot me a glance. I lifted a shoulder and dropped it. I wasn't about to take over the interrogation from him. The clock on the wall ticked away the seconds on its way to half past three. A door slammed somewhere. Rain rapped like an impatient lover at the window. Ned worried his hat.

"Out with it, man." Kevin blew out a breath. "We don't have all day here. Did you kill Justice Harrington?"

Ned's head jerked up. "No! I wouldn't do something like that. But I saw who did."

THIRTY-NINE

"I STEPPED OUTSIDE FOR A BREATH OF FRESH AIR and a cigar Monday night." Ned's voice shook as he went on.

I wanted to ask at exactly what time. I kept my mouth shut and let him talk.

"Folks don't take kindly to the smell of cigars indoors," Ned continued. "But I heard voices. A gentleman's and a lady's. They weren't shouting, but it sounded like an argument." Ned swiped at his forehead with a folded handkerchief. "I peered around the corner into the alley to see Mr. and Mrs. Harrington facing each other, arguing."

"What were they saying?" Kevin leaned his forearms onto the desk.

"I couldn't hear. I never knew one could fight while whispering, but fighting was what they were doing."

I had heard whispered arguments before. What a shame Ned hadn't been able to make out the content of this one.

"Mr. Harrington turned his back on her and began to walk in my direction. That is, back to the opera house," Ned continued. "I didn't want him to see me, and I pulled my head in around the corner. Mrs. Harrington yelled, 'Justice, come back. You have to!' I looked again, and he still walked toward me. She raised a gun in both hands and—" His voice broke. He buried his face in his hands.

Kevin looked at me. I held a finger to my lips. We needed to wait until he was composed. A full minute ticked by. Ned still didn't speak.

"Ned," I said softly. "What did thee see?"

He raised his head. "She shot him in the back. Three times. I saw her murder her own husband." Twisting his hands, he searched my face, then Kevin's. The skin bunched around his haunted eyes. "How does someone do that?"

Was Ned telling the truth? I'd never known him to dissemble nor to be experienced in theatrical arts. He certainly appeared devastated by what he'd seen. But why hadn't he come forward immediately? Was he putting on an act deserving of the stage?

"Humans are capable of the worst, Mr. Bailey." Kevin glowered. "Let's start with you sitting on this eyewitness account for a full week

140

without coming forward. How do you explain such inaction? And absconding with the gun to hide it at your home instead of bringing the weapon here as any responsible citizen would have done?"

"I was wrong to hide the gun and in error for not coming forth." Ned pulled down the corners of his mouth, and his shoulders sank over his chest. "I had such high hopes for my new venture, and Mr. Harrington had received my proposal with enthusiasm. I'd hoped to convince Mrs. Harrington she would also want to work with me."

"Let me guess, Bailey," Kevin said. "You didn't convince her. She shunned you. It was you who killed Justice Harrington. You, who then hid the gun and made up these stories against a respectable lady foreigner because she rejected your entreaties." He stood, fists on hips, nostrils flared. "You're only here now with your fabrications because your plans are gone, you don't have a business partner, and you are without hope for a future."

"No!" Ned said. "That's not it at all. None of it. You have to believe me. Mrs. Dodge does." He looked at me. "Don't you, Rose?"

I waited a moment before speaking. "I am not sure what I believe. Kevin, thee might want to take thy seat again." It looked to me as if Kevin was about to make a possibly premature arrest. And a probably false one. "I have a few more questions for Ned."

Kevin cocked his head, regarding me, then nodded as if to himself. He lowered himself into his chair with a mighty creak.

"What happened after Luthera fired the shots?" I asked Ned.

"I quickly stubbed out my cigar and melted back into a corner of darkness as Mrs. Harrington ran past toward the opera house."

"She ran?" Kevin asked.

"Yes." Ned bobbed his head. "As soon as I couldn't see her any longer, I dashed to Mr. Harrington's side. I prayed maybe he'd only been wounded. But he was already gone. Dead." He swallowed hard. "As I said, I hoped to continue my vision for the future with Luthera Harrington. I picked up the gun and stowed it in my overcoat pocket. I wanted to regain my plans, but I heard footsteps and hightailed it back to the opera house."

"And the next morning thee hid the gun," I said.

"I did."

"Think carefully now," I said. "Did thee see or hear anything else while thee was outside that night?"

141

He knit his brows. "Someone coughing. A man, I think."

Coughing. "What time is the closing event today?" I asked Ned.

He looked at the clock. "It starts in ten minutes."

I focused my gaze on Kevin. He returned it. He clasped one wrist with his other hand, then mirrored the action, eyebrows raised, mimicking the act of handcuffing.

I gave a quick shake of my head. "Not yet, I think. You and I need to get over to the event with all due speed. Someone must keep an eye on Ned here for the time being."

"But I need to —" Ned started to rise.

Kevin stood. "No, Mr. Bailey, you don't. What you need to do is sit right there while we confirm a couple of facts." He glared until Ned plopped back down.

FORTY

KEVIN DIRECTED AN OFFICER TO GUARD NED. On our way out, the detective shouted at a young officer to accompany us and directed another to bring the wagon around to the opera house with great haste and wait for us. We then rushed around the corner, as it was quicker to walk than wait for a police vehicle and horse to be readied.

"I didn't get a chance to tell you, Miss Rose," Kevin said as we hurried. "I'd queried a police contact up in Ottawa. I got a return telegraph today, saying Mrs. Harrington is some kind of markswoman. A sharpshooter. Canada's own Annie Oakley."

My breath rushed in. "So she's good with a gun."

"Very. She's won prizes."

The diminutive Oakley was famed the world over for her prowess with a rifle and for teaching other women to shoot. I'd read she had married Frank Butler in Windsor, Ontario. Had they also journeyed to Ottawa? Perhaps Luthera had been taught by the best shooter on the continent, lady or otherwise. I wished I'd had this information earlier.

Breathing heavily and reeling from all the sudden news, I followed Kevin into the opera house. Ned had most surely done the right thing by showing up at the station and reporting to Kevin. Doing it sooner would have been better, but thus it was. Thus all of it was. Now we had to find Luthera.

Inside, we both halted. The large foyer was packed with people. The double doors to the theater were closed, but a number of people seemed to be moving up the staircases on both ends of the building. A huge ballroom occupied the third floor, one often converted to a meeting space for purposes precisely like this one. I scanned the light-haired heads I saw, at least the female ones, and the black dresses. I didn't spy Luthera. I did see Georgia Clarke, who gave me an enthusiastic wave from across the foyer.

"I don't see the lady," Kevin muttered. "Do you?"

"No. Shall we go up?"

Kevin nodded. "Don't leave this door, hear?" he told the young policeman.

"No, sir. I won't, sir."

"If you spot Mrs. Harrington, detain her," Kevin added to the wide-eyed fellow. "She doesn't leave, and she doesn't go farther in. She might be a murderess."

"Excuse me, sir. I don't know what the suspect looks like."

I hurried to describe her and how she was likely dressed.

"Yes, ma'am." The young fellow nodded so hard I thought his neck might hurt later.

"Shall we, Miss Rose?" Kevin gestured to the right toward the less crowded of the two sets of stairs.

I considered suggesting we split up but thought the better of it. I began to follow him, weaving through locals and visitors talking in small groups. I overheard snippets of conversation. "Weather is such a pity," and "Murderer still at large," were among them.

I halted. William Parry stood with arms akimbo in a corner next to the stairwell. He scanned the crowd. I grabbed Kevin's elbow. He whirled.

I pointed and whispered, "Come with me." I wove through the crowd until I stood in front of William.

"Good afternoon, William."

He blinked, then looked sharply left and right as if for an escape route. Kevin and I closed in.

"A witness puts you on the scene the night of Justice Harrington's murder." Kevin scowled. "Why did you conceal what you knew?"

I whipped my head to look at the detective. This was not the approach I would have taken. Still, it was his case, not mine.

"Naturally I was there." William's voice rose. "What nonsense is this?"

"Was thee in the alley?" I asked more gently.

"No. Pardon me." He turned his head and coughed into a handkerchief. "As you both can tell, I am not well. I was seized by a paroxysm that evening and absented myself to take some fresh air. I stepped into the passageway next to the building."

Kevin opened his mouth for further bluster. I held up a hand to him. The passageway led to the alley.

"Truthfully now," I said. "Did thee witness a cry, a shot, anyone fleeing? Thee must help us."

William searched my face. He swallowed. "I heard steps running.

Light heels, like a lady's, in the alley behind the opera house. When I was about to go back in, I saw Mrs. Harrington. She was breathing hard as she shut the door behind her."

"Why didn't you go to the police with your information?" I asked.

"I didn't think it was important."

Or he didn't want her implicated in a crime, because he desperately needed an influx of money to save his company?

"We have to find her," Kevin murmured next to my ear.

I pointed upward. Kevin pushed through the crowd toward the stairs. William stared after him.

"Excuse me," I said to him and made to follow the detective.

"Mrs. Dodge, wait." William touched my arm.

I faced him. "Make it quick."

"Do you think she killed her husband?" He didn't speak softly and drew stares from others nearby.

When I stared back, they averted their eyes and hurried on upstairs. "That's entirely possible," I said to William.

"There goes that plan," he mumbled. His plan to rescue his business.

"If you'll excuse me, I need to find Luthera."

"But, Rose, you won't," Georgia said, suddenly at my elbow.

"Why ever not, Georgia?" I asked. "She's been here all week despite her mourning."

"Because she packed up all her things this morning, and she's headed back to Canada."

My heart sank. "What train did she catch?"

"She hasn't yet, quite. It's the four thirty."

I sucked in a breath, spying the back of Kevin's blue coat halfway up.

"Kevin!" I shouted, not giving a care for what people thought. I pointed to the door. "Depot."

FORTY-ONE

KEVIN AND I CLIMBED OUT OF THE POLICE WAGON, which had driven us the few blocks to the train depot with bells clanging. The young officer had come along, too. Kevin asked the man driving to stay and be at the ready.

This wasn't a large station, as Amesbury was the end of the line. The building, with its wide cantilevered overhang on all sides, had only recently been moved here to the corner of Elm and Water. The engine of a Boston & Maine passenger train sat huffing and ready on the tracks.

Kevin again ordered the young officer to post himself at the door and watch for any well-dressed light-haired ladies hurrying out. We pushed through the crowd inside to the platform. A conductor stood checking tickets and helping women up the two steps into the first car.

"Police," Kevin said to him. "Did a lady with a through ticket to Canada already board?"

I stepped forward. "She might have been dressed in widow's black." Or perhaps not. She'd be traveling among people who didn't know of her husband's death, and she obviously wasn't actually mourning. Luthera could have dressed in the garments she'd brought.

"Let me think, now." The conductor rubbed his forehead. "Why, yes, that lady. She's checked through to Montreal."

"Out with it, my man," Kevin said. "Which car is she on?"

"They're all the same. No first class on this train. Not until she transfers in Portland. She could be in any of the five."

Kevin rolled his eyes. "Come on, Miss Rose. You start here, and I'll run down to the other end and meet you. If you find her first, detain her until I get there."

"Now, hold on a minute," the conductor protested. He pulled out his pocket watch. "Train's due to leave in two minutes."

Kevin glowered. "Until Mrs. Dodge and I have descended with a known murderer in custody, train doesn't leave Amesbury."

The gent's eyes widened. "With all due respect, sir, that's not possible. We have connecting schedules to keep up. One late train and the entire network goes all to . . ." He glanced at me. "To heck."

"Kevin, we can get off in Newburyport," I blurted. The train from Amesbury had to first go slightly southeast to connect with any through lines, whether they traveled north or south. "It will arrive there in, what, twenty minutes?" I asked the conductor.

"Fifteen," the man said.

"Very well." Kevin sounded exasperated but took off for the caboose end of the train.

"Mrs. Dodge."

I turned to see a breathless Mary Chatigny at my elbow. She was dressed for traveling in a sturdy brown suit and duster, and she carried a full satchel.

"Mary, is thee taking this train?"

"Yes. I'm late, but I'm off to a medical conference in New York City." She lowered her voice. "What's this about a known murderer?"

I matched her tone. "I can't go into detail but, yes, there's a woman from Ottawa aboard who was responsible for this week's homicide."

A steely look came into her eyes. "How can I help?"

I liked this woman. "If thee sees a lady with pale skin and light hair, about my age and height and wearing stylish clothing, please engage her in conversation." My words tumbled out even as I saw the conductor check his watch again. "The chief and I will be going through the cars from opposite ends."

"I think I've seen her around town. I shall board in the middle." She strode down to the third car and climbed on without any help.

I smiled to myself at her fortitude as I ascended onto the first car, accepting the conductor's offer of a hand up. He fastened the heavy chain across the opening after me.

I opened the door to the car, gazing down the length of it. This local line didn't pull Pullman sleeper cars nor was it a luxury express train such as the one David and I had ridden to Cape Cod after our marriage, which had included lush upholstered chairs. The benches here were of a more utilitarian varnished wood.

A thought struck me. What if Luthera had been gazing out a window on this side and seen Kevin and me arrive? Or spied him racing down the platform to the other end. Would she have hurried to descend from, say, the second car and find her way out of town by some other means? Would the conductor apprehend her? I leaned my head back out and glanced up and down, but I didn't see her. If she had already made her getaway, perhaps the police officer at the depot door would nab her, but that depended on him recognizing her. It also depended on Luthera not talking her way out of being detained.

The conductor climbed on. "All aboard," he cried, leaning out from the passage between the first car and the coal car. The whistle blew, and the wheels began to move.

I tried to still my racing heart as I moved through the aisle at a funereal pace, checking each seat for Luthera. The train picked up speed and clacked through the woods toward Salisbury. It occurred to me the murderer might have disguised herself. Or perhaps she wore a traveling hat with a veil.

Spying someone I knew, I paused. Marie Deorocki huddled next to a window, a handkerchief to her mouth. Her shoulders heaved in a muffled cough.

"Where is thee bound, Marie?" I asked.

She glanced up, startled. "Hello, Rose. Dr. Chatigny convinced me I really must seek the cure at Saranac Lake."

"I wish thee safe travels and much healing, Marie."

She held up a hand in acknowledgment even as she bent over in a paroxysm of coughing. No wonder the seat next to her remained vacant. She couldn't get to the sanitarium a minute too soon.

I continued on my quest. At the far end of the car were sets of seats facing each other. After I passed, I peered at the backward-facing ones. No Luthera.

Pulling open the door, I stepped onto the overlapping iron plates of the noisy open space. The connected plates were designed to slide under each other when the train took curves. I caught myself on a vertical bar when the train swerved as it turned south. We now approached the railroad bridge over the mighty Merrimack River. I held on tight. The chain across the openings on both sides was the only barrier between me and the tracks along which we raced.

I opened the door to the second car to repeat my slow stroll. Instead I was met face-to-face with Luthera herself. Glowering, she stepped toward me, forcing me back onto the iron plates. The door closed behind her.

"You're in my way, nosy midwife," she growled.

I swallowed and stood my ground. "Please excuse me, Luthera. I'm looking for a friend."

Her nostrils flared. "No, you aren't. You're looking for me. You and the bumbling police chief." She clasped my forearm with her left hand and pressed a gun into my neck with her right. "I'm finished with the both of you."

FORTY-TWO

THE STEEL OF THE BARREL PRESSED COLD INTO MY SKIN. My heart thudded. My brain raced. I would not let her kill me. Nor my baby. I swallowed down my nerves.

"It would be a grave mistake to shoot me." I gazed at her steely expression, her icy eyes. She had brought two guns to Amesbury? Probably. Kevin had said she was a sharpshooter. She might have even more with her. "There's no escape for thee if thee kills again."

She barked out a harsh laugh. "There's also no escape for me if I don't. I know you've been assisting the police." Her tone was deadly above the racket. Between the iron grip on my arm and the pressure of the gun, she forced me to take a step closer to the opening. Did she mean to end her own life at the same time?

When I glimpsed the water far below, my throat tightened. My legs trembled. It would be bad enough to be forced out onto the ground rushing beneath. Into deep water rushing out to sea? I wouldn't have a chance.

"They know I shot Justice," Luthera said. "What a name, eh?"

I opened my mouth to reply but shut it. Better to let her talk. The more time I could gain, the sooner Kevin would be here. I normally preferred to be self-reliant, to save myself. Right now? My baby and I would take all the help we could get.

"My husband treated me like every other man in my life has," she went on with downturned mouth. "Telling me what to do. Bullying me in the guise of acting as my protector. Going behind my back to talk with that foolish man about his foolish plan."

"Ned Bailey's horseless carriages?"

"Yes. It's a ridiculous idea," she spat. "Montgomery Carriage is mine to do with as I wish. Not my husband's."

"I'm sorry thee hasn't been treated well." And I was. I was more sorry Kevin hadn't gotten here yet.

"My own father could teach a course in how to be a bully. Or could have. He's dead now," she crowed.

"That sounds like a painful upbringing." I thought she lessened the pressure on my neck a little. Maybe in her musings she'd forgotten her plan to push me into the river below. "Thy mother didn't shield thee from his treatment?"

"Mother? She was cowed and weak. And then she died giving birth to my baby brother. He died, too, and I became Father's heir apparent. Up until last year he still tried to run roughshod over me. I wasn't having it, Mrs. Dodge."

Had she killed her father, as well? It wouldn't surprise me, not with what I now saw of her.

Behind her, the door opened inch by inch. *Kevin.* I forced my gaze onto my attacker. I couldn't let on to Luthera that my rescue had arrived. Except in the periphery I spied not a serge uniform but a woman's bowler, decorated with a blue ribbon, atop still-blond hair.

The good doctor — Mary Chatigny — held a finger to her lips.

I mustered a response to Luthera. "Thee was right and brave to stand up to thy father."

Mary let the door slide shut. If it clicked, the noise of the wheels on the tracks concealed the sound.

"Of course I was." Luthera pulled the gun away from my neck and gestured her righteousness.

That was all Mary and I needed. From behind, Mary grabbed the wrist of Luthera's gun-holding hand and held tight. I raised my fist and socked the Canadian in the nose. She cried out, crumpling to the floor even as Mary twisted her forearm up. The gun fired into the open air beyond as it clattered down. It kept going through a gap in the plates, on to the river below.

"Nice work, Doctor," I said to Mary before sucking on my bruised, bloody knuckles. I'd never hit anyone before. Violence was counter to all the teachings of Friends. I thought God might forgive me, just this once, in the interests of preventing further violent acts.

"Nice work, Midwife." Mary grinned at me even as she kept her iron grip on the whimpering Luthera's wrist.

Our captive took the opportunity to kick out at my ankle. I stepped back in the nick of time.

Kevin pulled open the door behind Mary. "Miss Rose, I—" He stopped abruptly, taking in the scene.

The nature of the clatter changed as we exited the bridge and returned to tracks laid over dry land. From the first car, the conductor called out, "Next stop, Newburyport. Newburyport, next stop." He pulled open the door behind me. A gasp was all I heard.

"Mrs. Dodge and I have things under control, gentlemen." Mary stared pointedly at the slender wrist in her grip. "Chief Donovan, care to take over here?"

FORTY-THREE

KEVIN GRIPPED THE ELBOW OF A HANDCUFFED LUTHERA. We three alit at the Newburyport train depot, the first to descend as we were already between cars. I'd thanked Mary heartily and wished her a peaceful conference before stepping down with the help of the conductor. The doctor would continue on this train south. Blessedly the rain had ceased, but a stiff wind had blown it out to sea, and I shivered.

Rather than snarl and fight, Luthera had gone as icy as her eyes. "I demand to speak with the Canadian consulate in Boston." Her face was streaked with dried blood from the wound I'd inflicted, but it hadn't affected her pride.

"We'll put through the call, ma'am, but it won't be 'til tomorrow," Kevin said with a touch of satisfaction in his voice. "Today's the Lord's day of rest, you know. You'll be comfortable in the Amesbury clink, I'm sure."

I very much doubted it. She lifted her chin and looked away. Passengers climbing down stared at us, widened their eyes, and hurried away. A worried-looking railroad man rushed up. He glanced at Luthera's hands secured behind her back and returned a concerned gaze to Kevin.

"Call the Amesbury police station, my man," Kevin directed. "Tell them Chief Donovan needs the wagon here with all due dispatch, plus the matron."

"Yes, sir." The man hurried off.

Their only female officer would have to watch Luthera until she could be dispatched to the county lockup in Middleton. I wanted to call Faith, too, as soon as I arrived home. She would need to hurry to write her exclusive story.

"Do you have anything to say for yourself, Mrs. Harrington?" Kevin asked.

Luthera kept her gaze fixed on the roof of the depot and her mouth firmly shut.

I wanted to tell Kevin what she'd said about her husband and her father maltreating her. And give him a word about checking into how her father died. But I couldn't very well do so with her elbow in his grasp. Tomorrow would suffice.

"What will happen to Ned?" I asked Kevin in a soft voice, not caring if Luthera heard. I rubbed my bruised fist. Helping to stop her had been worth even more bruises than this one.

He let out a long breath. "The idiot obstructed justice. I'd like to see him serve a bit of time for it. But with the name of his family behind him, I doubt he'll be charged with much more than a hand slap."

I thought through the others he—and I—had suspected. Zeb was in the clear, as I knew he would be. William had done nothing wrong in the end. Prudence had come forward with her information.

"What about Jorge?" I asked. "He stole plans off a dead man."

"He'll probably not see much time, either, although he needs to return those papers to Mr. Bailey."

"Good." Would motor-powered carriages be in our near future? They would if Ned had anything to do with it.

The whistle of the northbound train from Boston split the air, and again, growing closer. The clack of wheels grew louder. A conductor holding a flag strolled to the front of the platform, ready to signal the engineer driving the train.

Luthera tore out of Kevin's grasp and ran for the edge of the platform.

"Stop that woman!" he cried as he dashed after her.

Perhaps Kevin had loosened his grip. Maybe I had overly distracted him, or he'd thought Luthera would remain compliant. I watched, aghast, as she paused for a second at the verge, preparing to leap onto the tracks at the last moment, when it would be too late for the engine to stop.

The conductor whirled. He whacked her back away from the edge with his flag. With her hands secured behind her back, her balance was off. She cried out and fell onto her back on the rough boards of the platform. The conductor stepped near her, the stick of the signaling device raised like a weapon. She tried to scoot nearer the edge to no avail, her mobility hampered as it was.

Kevin arrived, breathing heavily, his police weapon now drawn and pointed at her. "Don't you dare make a move, Mrs. Harrington."

Her nostrils widened as she glared, but she obeyed, not even moving her lips to speak.

"Thank you, sir," Kevin told the conductor.

"Can't have ladies leaping to their death," the conductor acknowledged. "Not on my watch, we can't."

The train huffed to a stop at the same time as the Amesbury police wagon pulled up. The matron climbed down from it.

"If you'll excuse me?" the conductor asked.

"As you were." Kevin's voice was gruff with chagrin. He yanked Luthera to her feet and marched her to the back of the wagon. After she was secured inside and in the custody of the matron, he put away his weapon and turned to me. "I'm sorry you had to go through any of this, Miss Rose."

I touched his arm. "All's well that ends well, Kevin. Right?"

"I suppose."

Bertie rode up on Grover. "Have we had some excitement here, Rosetta?" She grinned, pointing at the wagon after staring at my bloodied hand.

"After a fashion." I smiled up at her. "Luthera tried to shoot me on the train."

"Ooh. She's the murderer, is she?"

"Apparently. But Mary Chatigny and I managed to outsmart her."

"And the ladies save the day once again," Bertie said. "I like that. Do you know what Annie Oakley said? 'When a man hits a target, they call him a marksman. When I hit a target, they call it a trick. Never did like that much.'" She raised an eyebrow. "I guess Mrs. Harrington shooting her husband to death wasn't any trick."

"No, it wasn't." I stared at the wagon. "And she might have killed her own father, too."

Kevin snapped his head to look at me. I only nodded.

"Good afternoon, Detective," Bertie said. "Or, more rightly, Chief."

"Miss Winslow."

"I'm just back from a jaunt. How about a ride home?" she asked me. "Grover's as happy to carry two lovely ladies as one."

"In your condition?" Kevin frowned at me, then glanced at the wagon. "Wouldn't you rather sit in the front with the driver and me?"

"I'm pregnant, Kevin, not ill."

Kevin cast his eyes skyward. He knew me too well to question such an apparently odd notion.

I laughed. "Thank thee, but no. I'll travel back with Bertie." My friends had been turning up at all the right moments this week, for which I was grateful.

"Good." Bertie directed Grover over to a mounting block and slid off. "I think Rose and I have some catching up to do."

"Pay me a visit tomorrow," Kevin said. "We'll go over any unsolved bits, shall we?"

"I shall." I smiled at my partner in crime, so to speak. "Although it seems things are pretty well solved."

"I expect so," he acknowledged. "Thank you, Miss Rose, for your . . . well, for everything."

I waved goodbye as he climbed into the front of the wagon. Turning to Bertie, I said, "I think it might be prudent for me to ride sidesaddle for once."

EPILOGUE

DAVID NESTLED ATOP THE BED'S QUILT next to Hattie and me on this early Seventh Month afternoon. Our baby daughter, only five hours old, slept cradled in my arm. Her dark hair was finer than silk and as soft as a breeze. David stroked her cheek.

"Welcome to the world, Harriet Orpha Dodge," he murmured.

"Isn't she perfect?" We'd named her for my late sister, and for my late mentor. I looked forward to sharing stories about both women with Hattie as she grew. They'd been two of the most important people in my life.

"She's as perfect as her mother," David murmured. "You were a champion, Rosie."

I smiled at him. Annie had left only an hour earlier after cleaning up and making sure the baby and I were well and settled. Hattie had had a good first suckling, too.

"I was lucky. My body did what it was built to do." My pains had started in the wee hours of the morning, as so many do, but, unlike with many first-time mothers, it wasn't a prolonged labor. Orpha's deathbed prediction had blessedly come to pass. Hattie had entered the world at eleven fifteen this morning, with her father at my side. "Thee didn't mind I wanted thee with me?"

"I wouldn't have had it any other way. I know it makes me odd among those of my sex. But you and I, Rose, we made this little girl together. I wanted to be with you when we greeted her. It's not like I've never seen a baby be born."

"No, it isn't." I laughed softly. "Husband, dear, I remark that thy headaches seem to have vanished. I am glad."

"Yes, they have. I think I was worrying too much. About you, about the pregnancy. And, to be honest, about you being in danger. I didn't want to keep you from your need to see justice done, but I was concerned."

"Rightfully so."

Faith popped her head in. "Can I bring tea, water, anything?" She had come to relieve Annie and to meet her new niece.

"Thank thee, Faith. I am fine."

David kissed the top of Hattie's head and then the top of mine. "I'll let you girls have a visit. I need to get supper on."

Faith watched him go, then took his place next to me. "Thee found a treasure in that one." She stroked Hattie's tiny, perfect hand.

"And I know it."

"Hello, dear tiny cousin," she said to Hattie, then gazed at me. "Rose, I have news for thee."

I gazed back, suddenly suspecting what she had to say. I waited for her to share it.

"Zeb and I are going to have a baby, too." She brought both hands to her mouth, her eyes sparkling above them.

"Oh, Faith. I am so very happy for thee." My eyes brimmed and overflowed even as I smiled.

"Why does thee cry, Rose?"

I laughed, sniffing. "Emotions after childbirth go on a crazy trolley ride. I've seen it in the mothers I care for. Now I'm experiencing it. There's nothing to worry about." I took off my glasses and swiped at my eyes. "I daresay thee is due, let's see, about Christmastime, or in First Month?"

She nodded. "Thee will be my midwife, won't thee?"

"I wouldn't have it any other way. I'll need to have this little bug along, but Annie will assist, and we can get Betsy to watch Hattie between feedings."

"Nothing would make Betsy happier. She's been beside herself, as thee well knows, waiting for Hattie's arrival. Next year she'll have two little ones to care for—one a cousin and one a niece or nephew."

The doorbell rang downstairs, followed by murmured male voices. Two sets of feet tromped up. David, clad in an apron, stepped in looking worried.

"What is it, my dear?" I asked.

"Kevin is here. He didn't know you'd given birth, and he'll go right away if you say."

I surveyed myself. I wore a clean nightdress, with the quilt pulled up to my lap. I wasn't in pain, and the baby was sleeping. "Faith, please hand me that light shawl." I thanked her and wrapped it loosely around my shoulders. "I'd love to see him, and he can give Hattie one of his Irish blessings."

Kevin stepped around the corner of the doorway, hat in hand, cheeks flushed. "Here and you've given birth only today, Miss Rose. May I offer my heartiest congratulations?"

"Please, and thank thee. Come closer and see our girl. I'm decent enough."

He crept forward and peered at Hattie, but kept his hands clasped behind his back. "Well, by the saints she's a sweet one, and as pretty as they come." He straightened and spoke a string of words in Irish. "It's what we say for new babbies. 'May strong arms hold you, caring hearts tend you, and may love await you at every step.'"

"That is lovely." I tilted my head. "Now Kevin, since thee didn't know we had a new baby to bless, might I ask why thee stopped by?"

The detective rubbed his hair, as he had a habit of doing when things weren't going well. "It's this way. You probably haven't heard, but a man has been found dead near the Salisbury Point rail stop, and another man's gone missing. It looks like homicide, and the details of the case are confounding me something fierce."

"And thee wants my help."

"Rather desperately," he said.

I didn't look directly at David across the room. "I wish thee the best of luck with it. But I'm going to take a break from investigations."

"I was afraid you'd say so," Kevin admitted. "And naturally I wouldn't want you out traipsing around. But what if I only consulted with you about the facts? You're so good at helping me sort out my addled thoughts."

I gazed fondly at him. I would miss helping the police, being a sounding board, teasing out the facts with Kevin, and digging around asking questions in places he either couldn't venture or hadn't thought of.

"My answer is still no." I stroked Hattie's head. "What with motherhood and midwifery, I'm afraid even talking about murder would be too much." At least for now.

David blew me a grateful kiss.

"You know how invaluable your insights and assistance have been to me in the past," Kevin said.

"I thank thee for acknowledging my help. But I can't continue at this time."

Kevin clapped his hat on his head. The act was a final one, but his expression was kindly. He was a father of two. He knew what my life held going forward. "Very well. I do understand."

"I am glad." I didn't want David's headaches to return. I didn't want to do one thing to imperil Hattie's life or mine. I didn't know what would happen in the future. Perhaps I'd return to investigating homicides, perhaps not. For now, the light in my life had changed, gained a new focus, and I was at peace with it.

ACKNOWLEDGMENTS

Amesbury resident Mary Chatigny was the high bidder at the Amesbury Carriage Museum auction to have her name included in this book. Thank you for supporting our wonderful historical museum, Mary, and I hope you like your made-up historical self. When I told Mary her character would be a tuberculosis doctor, she was astonished, saying her grandmother had died of the disease in 1921. For the record, I have no knowledge of real Mary's vices, minor or major, and expect she has neither.

I enjoyed bringing back into this book other Amesbury residents whose names earlier appeared as characters because of their donations to worthy local charities. Thank you to Marie Deorocki (sorry about the TB, Marie), Fran Eisenman, Amy and Jonathan Sherwood, and Cathy Toomey for your generosity as well as your eagerness to see who you might have been in the late nineteenth century. Jeanne Papka Smith, a fellow Amesbury Quaker (and a fellow California Scorpio), simply donated her friendship to me and her lifelong experiences living as a blind person.

I purloined the name Luthera from my dear friend Deb Hamilton. Luthera was her great-great-great aunt, and a woman to be reckoned with. As far as I know, the real Luthera never had any involvement with homicide, but the name was too good not to use. I also borrowed the name of the great Brazilian author Jorge Amado for a visitor to Amesbury in the book.

Many thanks to midwife Risa Rispoli for reviewing the birth scene in this book, as she has in all the previous Rose Carroll mysteries. My own experience teaching and helping birthing mothers (and being one) was decades ago, so I'm always happy for a sanity check on unmedicated births. Thanks, too, to author-pal Áine Greaney for the Irish phrases about somebody who is not all there upstairs.

Kept company by my sisters Janet Maxwell and Barbara Bergendorf, I was blessed with the chance to sit with our mother, Marilyn Muller, as she died in April 2012. It is an honor to accompany a loved one—or anyone—on their last journey. I hope my sisters will forgive me for bringing some of my memories from that evening into a scene in this book. I also included a bit of my dear friend Annie Tunstall in Orpha's final days. Annie, one of my biggest fans, was bedridden in her last months. I was blessed by her intelligent company and her broad smile when I visited and helped in the smallest of ways, including feeding her when it became too painful for her to do so herself.

I'm grateful for Bill Harris and the team at Beyond the Page Publishing, who have published the most recent Quaker Midwife Mysteries. Thanks also to my agent, John Talbot, for connecting me with Bill.

I hold enormous gratitude for the late Ramona DeFelice Long, who led the seven o'clock online Sprint Club, a group of writers who all start the morning with an hour of focused creativity. Ramona gave each book in this series a deep read and enriched them in so many ways with her insightful suggestions and critiques. I couldn't have done it without her. She wasn't able to read this manuscript, and my fingers are crossed that I didn't miss something glaring. To my great sorrow, Ramona passed away while this book was in production. The Sprint Club continues in her honor, and I know how happy she would be to know Rose is pregnant and gives birth in this book.

I'm ever thankful to my fellow Wicked Authors, *aka* my support crew. Readers, please join us over at wickedauthors.com and meet these fabulous authors: Jessie Crockett, Sherry Harris, Julie Hennrikus, Liz Mugavero, and Barbara Ross (and all their alter egos).

Love always to my friends and family, to Hugh, and to my fellow Amesbury Friends for your support and joy at my successes.

I hope readers will also find my short stories, as well as my two contemporary mystery series, which I write as Maddie Day. Please remember, if you like a book, writing a short positive review and telling everyone you know is the best way to help the author.

Finally, thank you to all the dedicated fans of my fictional Quaker midwife. I've decided to let her move on with her life and let myself move on to new projects. The characters, era, and setting of this series have always been near to my heart, so don't be surprised if Rose pops up again in a short story now and again. Thank you for supporting Rose and gang all the way through.

About the Author

Agatha Award-winning author Edith Maxwell writes the Amesbury-based Quaker Midwife historical mysteries, the Lauren Rousseau Mysteries, the Local Foods Mysteries, and short crime fiction. As Maddie Day she writes the Country Store Mysteries and the Cozy Capers Book Group Mysteries.

A longtime Quaker and former doula, Maxwell lives north of Boston with her beau, an energetic young cat, and an impressive array of garden statuary. She blogs at WickedAuthors.com and MysteryLovers-Kitchen.com. Read about all her personalities and her work at edithmaxwell.com.

CPSIA information can be obtained
at www.ICGtesting.com
Printed in the USA
LVHW031540261021
701602LV00008B/1494

9 781954 717008